I0616727

HAZAIAH'S HEAD

A NOVEL BY ORHAN MILOSHE

The Artless Dodges Press
www.TheArtlessDodgesPress.com
Cleveland, Ohio

The following is a work of fiction. Characters, names,
situations, events, and locations described in this novel are
the invention of the author's mind, or are used fictitiously.
Any resemblance to persons living or dead is purely
coincidental.

All Rights Reserved. Printed in the United States of
America. No part of this book may be used or reproduced in
any manner whatsoever without written permission of the
publisher.

Hazaiah's Head
a novel by Orhan Miloshe
ISBN 0981993923
EAN-13 9780981993928
copyright © 2011 Artless Dodges, Inc.
Published by The Artless Dodges Press
Cleveland, Ohio
www.TheArtlessDodgesPress.com

Cover design by T. Maven
www.TrashMaven.WordPress.com

for Tutu, unintentional Patron of the Arts

Also by Orhan Miloshe

I AWOKE IN A HOUSE AFIRE

Contents

Foreword

The Indecipherable Puzzle:
Thoughts on Miloshe, Kafka, and Body Parts

I have been struggling with how to best articulate my thoughts about this excellent novel. As a fiction writer, my rule of thumb for these moments (when I have arrived at a scene, event, or epiphany that I just can't get right) is to go to my bookshelf and find a similar moment artfully handled by a better writer, and figure out how its author achieved his or her effect. However, nonfiction - or perhaps I should say essay - is a medium in which I have less experience, and so I can't say with any authority that such a principle holds true across the form. It is, however, the approach with which I am most familiar, and so it is the course I'm set to run, for better or for worse.

Stavros Stavros, author of the excellent novels *The Sirens* and *The Sentimentalist,* writes that reading Orhan Miloshe (specifically Miloshe's first novel, *I Awoke in a House Afire*) is like reading "Kafka with an LSD chaser" (this comment has received the somewhat glib reply that, for many, reading Kafka is enough like reading Kafka with an LSD chaser, although I mention this only so that you don't think you're the first to say it). To me, there is something wonderfully and succinctly insightful in this estimation, and I think that any attempt to formulate one of my own would only pale in comparison. I will instead endeavor to articulate my own thoughts in light of this assessment, and in so doing achieve (I hope) some useful commentary on the subject.

"Like Kafka with an LSD chaser": reading through this statement for the second (or maybe the one-hundred and second) time I feel a nagging concern that from this statement some may take it that Miloshe is a "drug" writer in the tradition of Hunter S. Thompson or Denis Johnson. Though I can appreciate the dramatic attraction of Mr. Stavros' phrasing, I worry that to lightly toss off a comment linking Miloshe to this tradition is, in fact, a disservice. This is a drug, after all, most commonly associated with the youth movement in the middle and late 1960s and early 70s, and I fear that such phrasing may give some readers the false impression that Miloshe is a writer concerned with events pertaining to that time and movement.

I make the point that to link Miloshe to the youth movement - to call him a writer preoccupied with a given time or place - would be a disservice only so that I might make the ensuing statement that Miloshe is in fact precisely the opposite: he is a writer preoccupied with no no factual events, persons, or places, for (despite certain familiar constructs: schools, militaries, governments, religions) the world in Miloshe's novels is a world that has never been, and will never be: it is our own world a dozen (or perhaps a few dozen) shades off, a few (or perhaps a few hundred) degrees stranger. The world of Miloshe's fiction lies somewhere between realism and folklore, and it is this fluidity that defines it: we think we are reading a realist drama when suddenly we find ourselves reading a fairy tale; we think we are reading Swiftian satire when we discover that we are reading existential allegory.

A disfigured creature is kept in the center of a subterranean labyrinth, men live in the belly of a whale, sadistic monks torment their converts: Miloshe repeatedly (and masterfully) leads us through the familiar to the threshold of the bizarre, and the resulting sense is reminiscent not of a drug experience but rather - as Mr. Stavros himself mentions elsewhere in his commentary - of a sudden awareness of the world's inherent strangeness: a beholding of the absurd. Indeed: the fantastical elements here form a kind of heightened super-reality, a series of supernatural (or perhaps they would be better called hyper-natural) trials which can neither be understood nor overcome by his characters, but only endured; one is often put in mind of Kafka's Joseph K., and his many failures and frustrations among the administrators and officiants of his cryptic trial.

And now again I find myself echoing Mr. Stavros, but again feel myself hesitating, for what is it exactly that links Miloshe to Kafka? What defining quality in Kafka echoes in Miloshe? The question becomes: what makes Kafka Kafka?

The Franco-Czech novelist Milan Kundera has described Kafka's novels as "variants on the same situation: man in conflict not with another man but with a world transformed into an enormous administration" (*The Curtain*, Harper Perennial, 2006).

The administration in each of Kafka's three novels is expansive beyond reckoning, and utterly (despite their earnest and tireless efforts) indecipherable to Kafka's protagonists: Karl Rossmann, Joseph K., and K. the land surveyor. Elsewhere Kundera theorizes that the Kafka situation is a product of its time: that it was precisely the sudden proliferation of industry that occurred at the beginning of the twentieth century (and that industry's attendant hierarchical operations and administration) that put Kafka in mind of a vast, bureaucratized clockworks in which (and into which) an individual might be lost forever.

The crisis of a man lost at sea, the twofold victim of a shadowy antagonistic force and his own ignorance within (and against) it certainly resonates, and I doubt very much that a reader would be overstating the case to say that he or she recognized something of Rossmann or Joseph K. in Miloshe's Rousseau. However, it seems to me that - though Kafka is undeniably the godfather of this sort of novel in the modern canon - there is something else at work in Miloshe's prose that reaches somewhat further along these lines.

The question is not one of quality but of intent, for who is indicted in Kafka's novel? To whom does this gross and horrifying parody point? Taking Kundera at face value we say that Modern Society (with its overcrowding, its mechanization, its dehumanization) is surely the object of the caricature. Do we infer further? And if so, who is then on trial? Is it rather life itself, the universe, the indecipherable puzzle of being? Shall we say then that God (God being the name we give to all that lies beyond our understanding; the God of Job, who allows men to experience unfathomable and unjustified suffering) is behind this literary mask? Is God the final administrator in Kafka's bureaucracy?

If Kafka's final administrator is God, then the bureaucracy in each of his novels is accordingly the literary mask worn by indecipherable existence; if his final administrator is *not* God - if his aim is leveled only at the ills of his time - then the bureaucracy is only that, and belongs to the (I must say, for lack of a better term) narrower (though certainly no less profound) horror of Man in Civilization. If God (and again, I use the term figuratively, as a unified name for the existential unknown) is beyond the ken of Kafka's concern (if it is perhaps in Kafka's view irrelevant to the pragmatic concerns of Joseph K.'s immediate and dire circumstances, K.'s consistent frustrations, or Karl Rossmann's anxious and wild ride on the vicissitudes of chance) then I assert that the dissimilitude between Miloshe and Kafka is as defining as their shared characteristics.

This is my contention: that while Kafka restricts himself to the immediate, the pragmatic, the physical (if only in that he does not extend himself - within the text, and scholars and critics may make their own cases about his "true" intent or subtext - to the transcendent, the ethereal, the metaphysical) Miloshe's work is populated (and indeed, defined) by various trials perpetuated by an array of antagonistic parties, ranging from governmental and religious bureaucracies to indifferent nature itself. It is here that I make the statement that Miloshe has traveled further along those lines set down by Kafka: in Kafka's work man faces a *society* that has become an indecipherable puzzle; in Miloshe man faces a *world* (a world containing and including innumerable and conflicting ideologies, containing nature and society, containing administrations and anarchy) that confounds him with its unintelligible and arbitrary occurrences. In Kafka one man's life disappears against the backdrop of society-become-bureaucracy; in Miloshe one man's life disappears against the backdrop of existence, laid bare in all of its endless indifference towards him.

And it is precisely this quality that one finds in arresting abundance - finds so artfully captured and conveyed - in *Hazaiah's Head*. One feels in Miloshe's prose a profound ambivalence towards and about his characters, finds a disturbing and disorienting refusal to validate even the most sympathetic of their plights, an unwillingness to take a side or relent. By giving equal voice to any and all Miloshe homogenizes the novel's events and the characters' hardships to such a degree the "disaster on the bridge" - in which hundreds are killed in the gruesomest possible way - is given no more dramatic treatment (and is in fact given fewer lines) than the Royal Advisor's complaints that his advice often goes unheeded. In another novel, or by another author, such disregard for dramatic expectation might seem a failure or shortcoming. Rather, in Miloshe's work such homogeny is *exactly the point*: it is the assertive refusal of the "responsibility" (for lack of a better term) implicit (again, for lack of a better term) in the author's godlike ability: namely, the power to spare his characters these hardships and, by extension, to appease the reader's sense for fair play and justice, for appropriate retribution and satisfying resolution. Indeed, what we find in Miloshe is a willful rebellion against storytelling convention: imagine the story of Job, but an alternate version in which God is indifferent to the suffering He allows Job to endure, or is perhaps entirely unaware that His actions are causing Job to suffer.

One further point about this novel: if we say that *I Awoke in a House Afire* is preoccupied with the fallacy of the belief in the consistency of external circumstances and the philosophical conclusions one might draw from the revelation of this fallacy *as* fallacy (readers will recall that the novel's protagonist, Rousseau, falls prey to such wild and unrepentant and precarious reversals that he eventually reconciles himself to the belief that existence is a "frantic and terminal farce" whose random workings hold absolute authority and whose concern for him is nonexistent) then we might also say that *Hazaiah's Head* is likewise preoccupied with the fallacy of the belief in the consistency of *internal* circumstances, or more exactly: the fallacy of the belief in the sanctity of *one's own body*. The horror in *Hazaiah's Head* (and here I refer not to certain "horror story" elements present in the novel, but rather to the weightier horrors also in evidence) is the horror of the *body as object*: that we will become not body and soul but only body: body that will rot and stink, body that will linger comically lifeless, body that takes up space and must be dealt with. (And not only ourselves, but everyone we know and everyone we love, everyone to whom such an alteration seems an unbearable and impossible and unallowable atrocity: all of our objections, the novel repeatedly and deftly counters, count for nothing against this eventual inevitability.)

Again: when the executioners arrive and stab Joseph K. through the heart we know only that his absurd trial has come to an end, see only the system's final assertion that it owes no explanation to those it destroys. When, in the third chapter of *Hazaiah's Head*, we see a sudden chance accident leave dozens dead and further dozens grievously wounded, there is no ambivalent administrator to blame but only ambivalent existence: *existence* which owes no explanation to those its workings destroy (among whom we ourselves will one day be counted). Again, this is the soul of Miloshe's artistry: what at first glance reads as his ambivalence about and indifference towards his characters reveals, on closer reading, a profoundly humanist anxiety that existence regards man so indifferently; his indifference to his characters is *the world's indifference to us*, and those who feel themselves recoiling from his work might do well to reconsider their own expectations of a world in which men, women, children, criminals, police personnel, the innocent, the guilty, the somewhere in between, the un-extraordinary, the very busy, the lazy, those who "deserve it," those who don't - to whit: thousands of people from every possible walk of life - are daily and indiscriminately dispatched with in horrible and non-horrible ways, for no particular reason at all.

Ellison Fowler's work may be found at www.EllisonFowler.Wordpress.com. His first collection of short stories, **The Distinction of the Mature and the Horror of the Naive, and Other Stories of Youth in Limbo**, *will be published by The Artless Dodges Press in the fall of 2011.*

Author's Note

When We Become Cargo

I had the idea for the novel that became *Hazaiah's Head* while reading a news item regarding a cargo of "up to sixty" human heads (and what the article described as "partial heads") that had been seized at an Arkansas airport. No one knew, at the time of the discovery, the specimens' purpose: they had been erroneously labeled, and neither the shipping nor the receiving parties could be reached for comment by the time the story ran. Nor was the compartment refrigerated, or its contents kept on ice: rather the heads were packed, according to the coroner, "in regular plastic containers, and wrapped with water-absorbent material and duct tape."

I wrote my first novel, *I Awoke in a House Afire,* in an attempt to articulate what might be called a progress to a philosophy: a philosophy which I stated rather explicitly in the Creature's speech in Book Four and echoed in my protagonist's speech at the novel's end (it is from this speech, readers will recall, that the novel's title is derived). I had the same idea in mind when I was writing *Hazaiah's Head*. That philosophy (and the progress to it, for one is nearly inseparable from the other) go (in brief but not in full) something like this: the mystery - the "why" and the "what" - of human existence can never be satisfactorily reconciled; they elude man's understanding because man's (by nature, limited) vision and comprehension determine the (by necessity, limited) scope of his cognitive grasp. His (animal) mind skillfully forms a functional understanding of his immediate surroundings *as they relate to himself* (he is able, for example, to negotiate the relationship between a fruit tree and his own hunger), but beyond this (if he attempts, perhaps, to negotiate the relationship between the vast universe and the fruit tree that has risen, seemingly miraculously, from the earth) even the brightest minds among his race falter and fall silent. Certainly he is able to understand the tree's progress from seed to seedling, from shoot to plant, from immaturity to maturity! But ask him for what reason trees grow upon the earth, to what end life perpetuates, within what progress this phenomenon stands, and his answers become less sure; eventually he must (if he is honest) admit his ignorance.

Perceiving this parameter, his life takes on a familiar progress: horrified that he is, in effect, stumbling about in blind ignorance, he constructs every sort of explanation, which he then exalts into myth and calls sacrosanct. (In an attempt to placate those whom the following might offend, and in a further attempt to resist the temptation to testify on behalf of yet another credo, I will say that *in this view* the world's various religions, political systems, laws, and social ideologies are only artificial boundaries elevated to the realm of Objective Truth, by which process man attempts to assuage his horrified idiocy.)

For many, this first movement (from horror to dogma) comprises a full and satisfying psychological evolution: to these individuals the question is answered. If, however, an individual feels unsatisfied by any given answer, he may attempt instead to satisfy himself by exploring other answers offered in other parts of the world. If these too fail him, he may come to perceive that the only inalienable and indeed constant truth is that of his own imperturbable ignorance: that he is a man, and limited by nature; that his own assertions (or those of others), complete as they may be, being the product of his (or other men's) meager faculties, may never ordain to speak with the unimpeachable and final authority to which they aspire.

This insidious realization, unsatisfied with those conscious and intentional suppositions (by this I mean those suppositions decided upon by the rational mind: law, religion, et cetera), works backwards: soon he is compelled to the further realization that the subtle and precognitive coding with which he interprets - and reconciles himself to - every minute occurrence is likewise constructed of nothing (for his ignorance is boundless, and his assertions hold no authority). His world then begins to crumble before him, and its happenings to seem only as an absurd and farcical progress which can never be understood (for who is he to assert the meaning of any occurrence?) but only endured, until the moment of his death.

But in death, too, there lies a startling realization, for he must recognize that in all likelihood his death will be final and absolute, that nothing of him will endure, that all assertions of transcendence, immortality, human divinity, eternal life, reincarnation, et cetera, are the products of men and are likewise discredited by the simple fact of man's profound myopia (must realize also that even the desperate, pleading compulsion he feels towards them is in no way an indication of their truth). And it is here that the progress ends: man knows only that he knows nothing, that he can never know anything; that he is an animal like any other; that upon his death he will be received into an indifferent void, that his own coveted self - the precious star of his universe - will be effortlessly and eternally dissolved.

I was pleased with *I Awoke in a House Afire* for several reasons, not the least among which was my sense that I had successfully articulated this philosophy and, with some degree of art, illustrated my protagonist's progress to it. I did feel, however, that the philosophy warranted some further consideration and exploration which were unfeasible within the confines of a novel like *I Awoke in a House Afire*. More exactly, it was impossible to traverse that threshold comprising the philosophy's final (and perhaps, most important) movement in a story told by and centered around a first-person narrator (or indeed any narrative structure composed around a single protagonist, whether first-person or not).

This was my primary concern as I began work on the novel that became *Hazaiah's Head*: how to write a novel in which death - not merely of peripheral characters, but of integral components of the narrative landscape - could be folded into the fabric of the story in such a way that finality would be implied but action could continue. But how to wrangle continuation from finality? One (somewhat familiar) approach is to follow a first-person protagonist very nearly to the moment of his death (Camus' *The Stranger* comes to mind, and readers of *I Awoke in a House Afire* may note a substantial nod to the revered Algerian), and in so doing achieve some degree of the intended impact of so catastrophic (to the narrative, if not to us personally) a shift. But some brief consideration of this option soon revealed its shortcomings: even if I follow my protagonist to the very moment of his death the event forms a boundary beyond which I cannot proceed, and the novel is stopped short of its mark, and that which gives the philosophy its dire relevance is left up to the reader's imagination (and we are right back where we started, with finality but no continuation). True finality (the finality that one only senses when one observes that the rest of life, indifferent to the death, simply moves on) is impossible in this sort of composition. Nor did I find it suitable to write a novel in which a character continued speaking from beyond the grave: readers will no doubt agree that for my purposes this method was out of accord with the substance of the argument (for certainly one cannot ask a character speaking from beyond the grave to assert that one's life ends absolutely with one's death!). Nor was it feasible to write a "group novel," the sort centered around a small band of individuals, in which I might illustrate by the death of one member the substance of the philosophy. True finality (the finality of the world's ambivalence) is here impossible as well: such action in a "group novel" requires mourning, requires palliative (to the characters and to the readers) remembrances, and such (again) leave one with the (false) impression that death is not final, that some comfort might be taken in the prospect of immortality through memory.

Given that these avenues were unacceptable, it became clear to me that any sort of character-centered story would prove problematic in my efforts to express the latter half of the philosophy. It seemed then necessary, to some degree, to forgo the familiar narrative framework, and flout the Law of Constancy, and construct a novel centered around not an individual or group of individuals but rather a great number of individuals, each of which might, at any moment, for any reason, and in a variety of ways, die a final and inglorious death (and who, taken together, might by the sheer bulk of their collected corpses, the ease of their expiration, and the narrative's constant and amnesiac forward movement imply the effortless finality of this much-feared boundary).

This explains, I think, if only in broad strokes, the philosophical impetus for both *I Awoke in a House Afire* and the novel that became *Hazaiah's Head.* Something more might be said, however, regarding the content of this second novel (and I will here ask readers to recall the sixty-odd heads, waiting silently on the Arkansas tarmac)...

Of the movements that make up the previously-described progress I find it to be a most stupefying phenomenon that the body becomes something *apart from ourselves*, something foreign and *material*. I am fascinated by the confrontation between one's internal reality (one's beliefs, his reconciliations, his rationalizations) and his external circumstances: fascinated that an entire universe (all that one imagines he knows within the coded and ordered matrix of his perspective) can vanish so thoroughly and that the body, divested of this, becomes a *thing*. The sixty-odd heads contained within the shipment grounded in Arkansas stagger us with their sheer bulk: our interior reality seems to resist dissolution (how comforting and natural it is to imagine that a soul or spirit survives our physical expiration!); we find it difficult to imagine that any individual (with all of his elaborate social mechanisms, humorous anecdotes, fond memories, prejudices) simply ends; we find it harder still to imagine that we (with all of our social graces, our likes and dislikes, our funny stories, et cetera) will end. We say to ourselves: I (the protagonist of my life, the main character in this drama!) must certainly survive; if I do not, then some facet of my sacred self must endure. But what comes of this desperate assertion when the mind that birthed it - the eyes through which it observed its dire circumstances, the tongue with which it voiced its lament, the ears with which it sought some affirmative reply from reticent heaven - is gray and silent and lifeless, wrapped in plastic and piled beneath several dozen others, in a cargo container on the Arkansas tarmac? Or perhaps we say: at least let my death come only at the end of some proper and fitting dramatic build: let me expire only under heightened and poetically-appropriate circumstances (and in this way, perhaps, live on in the physically disappointing but no less psychologically comforting realm of myth). But no, life seems to say: the slightest and least poetic misstep can cause you disastrous calamity, which will surely pierce the illusory bubble you think surrounds you, and indifferently extinguish your spark. No, say the sixty heads on the Arkansas tarmac: your final worth is measured not in virtue and vice but in pounds and ounces...

But now these notes have exceeded their allotted role, have begun to testify on their own behalf. I will therefore say in closing that I am grateful to the people at The Artless Dodges Press for their unending support, enthusiasm, and - how shall I put it? - willingness to indulge my aesthetic. Literary fiction is never an easy sell (and sprawling, philosophical, genre-less fiction is a marketing department's nightmare), but nowhere in the course of bringing this novel to print did I feel any pressure to tailor my words to any standard save my own. The publisher's passion and seemingly limitless faith in its reading public is both rare and inspiring, and my gratitude toward them knows no bounds. I am also grateful, by extension, to those Clevelanders who, through their generosity and stalwart commitment to the arts, gave The Artless Dodges Press the freedom and ability to in turn give me the freedom I so enjoyed while working with them. Finally, and perhaps most importantly, I wish to express my gratitude to all of those unwitting patrons of the arts who made this book possible.

- O.M.

HAZAIAH'S
HEAD

1.
The Call

The call, arising from the Royal throat of the reclining King, possessed of a great bellow from his Royal lungs, propelled by his Royal vocal chords, passed his Royal lips with such fury as to fill the august and stately bedchamber, traverse the threshold into the hall without and escape, through the open-air congress, even into the central courtyard, where it echoed momentarily among the gilded domes topping the Castle's many towers, and disturbed as it did the many birds nesting there and startled the many guards on duty, before it rose, finally, into the blue and cloudless and insensate heavens.

"Bring me the head of Hazaiah the Terrible!"

"But Your Majesty," replied Hassock, the most trusted of the King's Advisors, emerging from behind the couch where he had, by force of habit, and owing to his now ruined nerves, reflexively hidden at the King's outburst, "perhaps we should think twice before taking so drastic a tact with so dangerous a man. After all, think of the stories! Hazaiah is not a man to be trifled with, and one should give careful consideration before seeking to make one such as him one's outright enemy. Imagine if, by some unforeseen occurrence, Hazaiah were to discover Your Majesty's plot! There is no telling how vast his network of support spreads within the populace. Think of the trouble he could cause! A civil conflict such as the one that might ensue would weaken our borders and leave us vulnerable to attack from without. And this, while new reports arrive daily of our enemies' massing warships to the south! And I hear rumors, Majesty, that scouts have been sighted crossing the Hridish Pass. Lastly, and perhaps most importantly, I must insist in the name of Your Majesty's health that Your Majesty refrains from such outbursts, and attempt at all costs to remain unperturbed, even in the most dire of circumstances. Your Majesty knows better than I what the Royal Doctors have said!"

"Hang the Royal Doctors," replied the King, lifting as he did so a rather large and heavily bejeweled bowl that sat on the bedside table and heaving it in the general direction of Hassock, the Most Trusted Advisor, who once again hid behind the couch. "And hang the stories as well! I am not some gullible child, frightened of stories! Hazaiah is a man like any other! Come out from behind there!"

Hassock, eyeing warily all of the objects within the King's reach, rose from behind the couch.

"I had no desire to upset You further, my Great and Beneficent King," he said, kneeling on the carpet beside the King's bed. "It is only that I fear what harm may come to Your Majesty! Imagine, Majesty, if Hazaiah is not immediately captured, and perhaps decides to level his arrows against the Crown! The boundless frustration such a conflict is liable to cause surely bodes ill for Your Majesty's health."

"Balderdash!" cried the King, raising as he did so a rather large and heavy-looking goblet (Hassock, somewhat immobilized by his posture, covered his head with his hands). "What do you mean, frustration? Are you suggesting that my assassins will be unable to complete so simple a task? No man may fail to achieve what their King asks of them!" and here he drank rather noisily from the cup.

"Of course," replied Hassock, the King's Most Trusted Advisor. "I meant only that..."

But here he halted his entreaties, for the King had begun to pull on a braided and tasseled cord hanging beside the bed, producing from the next chamber a cacophonous and discordant ruckus. No sooner had this noise ceased than the Royal bedchamber doors were thrown open and a phalanx of soldiers, visors lowered and spears raised, entered and surrounded the terrified Advisor.

"Majesty!" cried the terrified servant, prostrating himself further, "I beg your forgiveness! Whatever it is I have said to offend Thee, I wholly recant! Your Majesty's wishes are not to be questioned!"

"Idiots!" shouted the King. "Are you all so dim-witted as to mistake my Most Trusted Advisor for some assassin? And do you think I, your King, and therefore our nation's mightiest warrior, would be caught unawares by an enemy, and remain couched within my bedsheets? Lower your spears at once!"

The soldiers lowered their spears. The Captain of the Guard, raising his visor, knelt before the King and bowed his head, the very image of contrition. Hassock, overjoyed by the sudden change in circumstances, rose and pushed the nearest soldier who, being somewhat unbalanced and clumsy in the bulky armor he wore, fell violently into the soldier behind him with a terrific crash.

"My Liege," said the Captain of the Guard, raising his voice to be heard over the clamor of the felled soldiers, "I humbly beg Your forgiveness. So great is my love for my King, that I leapt forward with little consideration for my life or the lives of my men."

"As you should," replied the King.

"Accordingly," continued the Captain of the Guard, "I paused not at all in my headlong flight to consider the circumstances upon which I had entered, so certain was I already that my beloved King was in mortal danger."

"A forgivable misstep," said the King approvingly. "Only a fool of a king would punish such blind loyalty. Arise, with your King's thanks."

The Captain did so, eyeing Hassock, the King's Most Trusted Advisor, who under the imposing man's gaze retreated somewhat closer to the King's bedside.

"Now," continued the King, swinging his feet over the edge of the bed and sitting up, pushing Hassock (the Most Trusted Advisor) out of his way as he did so, "your King commands you! The Lord Hazaiah, sovereign of our most remote and barren and worthless region, provider of a pittance of a tithe, sometimes called Hazaiah the Terrible, often called Hazaiah the Wretch, so long a thorn in the side of this Kingdom, a burr under Its saddle, an ingrown nail on the foot of the Monarch, a tick under Its collar, a child tying Its bootstraps together under the dining table, long suspected of subversive activity against the Crown, widely believed to be responsible for the attacks which occurred on the twelfth of September last, the fifth of June most recent, and the eighteenth of August two years gone, as well as innumerable lesser infractions, commander of the northern volunteer battalion, has drawn his last breath as a freeman! Your King demands the head of Hazaiah the Terrible!"

"Very good, Highness," replied the Captain of the Guard.

"Whoever brings it to me shall have his weight in gold!" continued the King.

"Very good, Sire," replied the Captain of the Guard, raising his voice slightly to be heard over the clatter from the rear as a pair of guardsmen, at the mention of this prize, left their posts and quit the room in a terrific hurry.

"And," went on the King, oblivious to this interruption, "he shall be appointed to my Cabinet of Advisors, and shall sleep every night for the rest of his days in the Castle's comfort, and shall never again want for anything."

"But Majesty," interjected Hassock, the Most Trusted Advisor, crawling upon the floor and moving from the King's path the various objects which the King, in his tantrum, had thrown about the room, and which threatened great injury to the King's unshod and thoughtless steps, "perhaps Your Highness should more thoughtfully consider such extravagant rewards! Think, Highness, of what sort of man is likely to win such a wondrous prize! Surely such a task requires someone ruthless, clever, vicious! Would You embrace a viper to Your Royal breast? As your Advisor I must advise strongly against this!"

This vehement polemic went unheard and unheeded, for as Hassock spoke the remainder of the guardsmen, in a fantastic hurry to reclaim the ground already lost to the first to leave, spurred on by the fantastic prize offered, exited the room in a great crashing and clanging of armor and spears. Their departure left a silence in which Hassock once again attempted to intervene on behalf of reason. This attempt, too, went unheeded, for as Hassock began again to speak a great trumpeting erupted from the courtyard without and the voice of Himdrigard, the Royal Herald, bellowed to all who might hear the particulars of the King's extraordinary proposal.

"Well, I suppose there's no use arguing about it now," said Hassock, quietly and to himself. "He's made His bed, sure enough, and now the rest of us have to lie in it." Then, rising from the floor, and considering the King (who had since returned to bed, and was now softly snoring) Hassock took his leave, his thoughts greatly troubled by all that had occurred.

2.
The Massed Legion

The massed legion, comprised equally of enlisted soldiers and mercenaries, numbering in the hundreds, armed with implements appropriate to each bearer's status and vocation, waited impatiently inside the massive portal while the equally massive drawbridge, its mechanism alternately jamming and unjamming, alternately sticking and unsticking, slowly descended. Without awaited several thousand of the wretched who farmed the unprotected lands beyond the stout wall and who, having no hope of bettering their circumstances, sought to align themselves (by Providence) with the winning contender, in this way ingratiating themselves not only to the recipient of the King's magnanimous prize but, each silently hoped, to the King Himself.

"Look at that one," said one of these wretched to another, even more wretched than himself, when the bridge had finally been lowered and the contenders emerged amidst cheering and general confusion. "I've never seen a man so large! Surely he'll be the one to win it."

"But look at the one behind him!" replied the second, wiping as he did an unhealthy-looking glob of something or other from a rather large sore on the side of his neck, up under his ear. "I'd say he's more fit to the challenge! Look how effortlessly he carries his battle club! No doubt it would take two ordinary men just to lift it!"

"Idiots!" joined a third, somewhat less wretched than the others but only, it was obvious, through great effort. "Such a task will take cunning and intelligence! Aligning yourselves with the biggest and the strongest will get you nowhere! A man's brains cannot be measured by his appearance!"

"Fine then," replied the first. "Tell us then: how will you pick which man to follow? You've no more way of knowing which man is best suited to the task than we!"

"Perhaps you are correct," replied the third. "At this moment I regrettably find myself in such circumstances as condemn me to an ignorance rivaling your own. But gentlemen, the potion with which one cures one's ignorance is surely not hasty action! By pursuing the course set upon by his own uninformed thoughts a man often condemns himself to the very course which later and more learned consideration eschews! I endeavor, therefore, to withhold my allegiance until more information finds its way vouchsafe to me."

"Oh, your allegiance," said the first, rolling his eyes. "Well, I certainly hope the rest of us are able to carry on, knowing that your allegiance is still unaffiliated. I suppose it'll be a wonder if the whole processional doesn't break down, and start squabbling about at your feet. Your allegiance is the prize, after all!" and here he burst out laughing with such unchecked violence as to send a great deal of white spittle flying from his lips.

"Oh, yes, squabbling at your feet," rejoined the second, wiping as he did so a bit more of the unhealthy-looking discharge from beneath his ear and laughing in a perfect imitation of the first.

"Simpletons," said the third, drawing himself up to his full height and recoiling, somewhat, at the grotesque theatrics being performed before him. "Why have you come, if not in the hope that you might better yourselves, might improve your circumstances? Now you see before you one who might achieve such a transformation, and you laugh and sport like apes! Spend your lives in the dirt for all I care!" and here he retreated into the crowd, clutching his cloak around him as though for fear that any contact with the mob might infect him with something terrible.

"What's wrong with him?" asked the first, when the third was gone.

"Who knows?" replied the second, now beginning to pick at the sore on his neck. "In any event, we won't be needing him. Look at the one coming our way! He's sure to manage the trick."

"I believe you're right," agreed the first. And, shouldering rather rudely into the crowd, they made their way toward the giant now exiting the castle, eager to make their allegiance.

3.
The Disaster on the Bridge

Just then a terrible accident occurred. The mechanism controlling the raising and lowering of the drawbridge, which had been alternately jamming and unjamming, and was in truth in sore need of maintenance, failed: the massive counterweights, suddenly loosed of their hinderances, plummeted to earth; accordingly the bridge, with all of its heavy steel and timber, was hauled suddenly home, sending dozens plummeting into the moat (where, clad in heavy and warlike raiment, several were drowned), sending many more hurtling back to the flagstones beneath the great gate (where some were crushed under the weight of the many bodies, while others were impaled on the various weapons there present), crushing several in the constriction between bridge and archway (and cutting many of these completely in half), and depositing fewer than ten upon the opposite shore (these ten, falling from a great and increasing height, did not escape injury, but rather displayed as they disentangled themselves broken limbs and sprained joints, and at least one deep and troubling puncture).

"What does it mean?" cried the gathered peasantry.

To which the clergy, in attendance to bless the endeavor, fervently replied. "God frowns upon this crusade!"

4.
The First Night's March

It was well past evening when the mechanism was restored to working order, and those trapped behind the Castle's great wall able to exit. The miserable and wretched, waiting beyond the wall, greeted the descending bridge and the exiting force with a great cheer which carried for several miles across the village without and the open plains surrounding. Numerous torches were lit from the innumerable fires that had been built during the delay, in whose flickering light the advancing warriors seemed monstrous and indomitable.

"Surely none can stand before such a force!" cried the wretched.

To which the attendant clergy, uncertain of the crowd's mood, remained silent.

"Forward!" cried the foremost warrior, a knight brandishing both lance and shield. And, spurring his charger, he set off across the plain at a terrific pace which the others, being on foot, could not hope to match.

"He'll be the first at the prize, there's no doubt," said one of the wretches to another. "And no chance to pledge my allegiance to him. Might as well go home now, I suppose."

"Not hardly!" replied the other. "Look there!" and here he pointed to another of the horde who, brandishing a great bow, let fly with a barb-tipped arrow which soared off into the darkness toward the still-distinguishable glint of the rider's armor.

"Not a chance," said the first.

"Shut up and listen," said the second.

Any resultant sound was, however, indistinguishable above that of the approaching mob, and the scene too far out of sight and too obscured by darkness for any conclusion to be drawn.

"Felled him, I'll wager," the second declared nonetheless, wiping his prodigiously running nose. "That's Hipuptup, the most deadly archer in the Kingdom. They say he never misses."

"Balderdash," replied the first. "I'll lay nine against."

"You haven't got nine to lay, either way," countered the second.

"You worry about your own nine," said the first. "Besides, at that distance, and in the dark, too, it shouldn't be my own nine we worry about."

This argument quickly devolved into baseless accusations and shouted insults, and soon the two had to be bodily restrained by those surrounding for fear that whatever fracas ensued (in the dark, and with so many weapons present) might unintentionally cause injury to some uninvolved bystander. Eventually the quarrelsome parties were convinced to settle their differences or go their separate ways, which they did with relish, flinging final barbs over the heads of those moving to form a barrier between them.

By this time the crowd advancing from the city had achieved and surpassed the mob gathered without, and those distracted by this argument were compelled to run after them. Several hundred yards further along the path they passed the felled body of a knight, an arrow lodged securely between helmet and corselette. The horse had run off somewhere, and could not be located.

"That's Hipuptup's work," the peasants murmured to each other, shaking their heads. "They say he never misses. He'll surely be the one to win the prize," and several dozen crowded around Hipuptup, pledging their allegiance and offering what base presents their meager circumstances allowed, and greatly inhibiting the progress of the march.

All hopes that Hipuptup would win the prize were dashed, however, when early in the morning hours one of the others (Hossososo, a member of the King's weekend bodyguard) made his way through the crowd still ringing Hipuptup and ran the archer through with his sword. A great moan of disappointment arose from those who felt they were making headway in their quest to ingratiate themselves to the favorite. This moan was mirrored by a cheer arising from the throats of all those who could not get close enough to Hipuptup to pledge their fealty, but now had a chance to kiss the feet of the new leading man. No sooner had these begun to prostrate themselves before Hossososo, however, than a great battle axe fell from out of the darkness, lodging securely in Hossososo's shoulder and chest. In the stunned silence that followed the bearer of this axe (a mercenary named Hunhungaroo) declared in a booming voice that all pledging of allegiances should cease, at least until a camp was made for the night, or the congregation would get nowhere.

"Look, you simpletons, you morons," he said, pointing back to where, to everyone's dismay and discouragement, the topmost lights of the castle were still plainly visible above the horizon, "We've been at it for hours, and barely moved at all. Would you prefer that we never get there, or that Hazaiah finds adequate time to prepare for our arrival? Walk forward and keep your mouths shut, you dullards, or my axe will have a few words for you."

This threat achieved its desired effect, for the crowd moved through the remainder of the night with great efficiency. At dawn they made camp atop a high hill overlooking the valley beyond which lay the Great Forest and the Infinite Lake, and the Mercurial Swamp, and finally, far beyond the horizon, the lands over which Hazaiah was Lord.

5.
Hipuptup and Hossososo

The axe, when removed from Hossososo's chest and shoulder, made an oddly comic slurping sound which caused the bearer of its injury, in insensate shock, to giggle, and to continue giggling long after the event which had produced the effect.

"What on earth could you possibly be giggling about?" inquired Hipuptup, after everyone else had gone, and the sound of Hossososo's giggling filled the vacant night (and with an unchecked note of annoyance in his voice, stemming not only from his genuine irritation at Hossososo's tittering but also his rather painful injury, and his hatred towards its author).

"Oh, I beg your pardon, nothing at all," replied Hossososo, rather startled. "You'll forgive me for saying so, but I had thought myself alone out here."

"Well you're not," snapped Hipuptup, making no effort to mask his hatred. "I'll thank you to consider my feelings on the matter, the next time you decide to go on making such a ludicrous racket."

"I'm terribly sorry," replied Hossososo. "I had no wish to offend."

"Well offend you have!" shouted Hipuptup, in an outcry whose effort immediately produced a rather violent fit of coughing and a bright red sputum which appeared on the speaker's teeth and lips, and spilled over across both cheeks.

"You'll forgive me for saying so," offered Hossososo, in what could only be called a conciliatory tone, "but you don't seem terribly well."

"I'm not well, you fool!" cried Hipuptup, restraining his spasming lungs with effort. "You've killed me! How well might I be? How well would you be, with three feet of steel shoved through your middle?" at which, unsheathing his dagger, and turning onto his belly, he made a brief and frantic attempt on the dozen or so feet which lay between them (Hossososo, having the use of only one arm, made an odd and crab-like retreat, posting with his good hand and kicking with both feet so that, scuttling, he was able to preserve the distance).

This pursuit was over in a matter of moments, for both men soon collapsed in exhaustion and pain. Their wounds, somewhat staunched by whatever garment lay atop them, bled anew. Hipuptup dropped his dagger and vomited; Hossososo, overwhelmed by the fresh burst of agony his violent retreat had produced, wept openly.

"Oh, stop that!" cried Hipuptup. "Crying won't do you any good."

"I know that," blubbered Hossososo, "but I can't help it!"

"It's all right," said Hipuptup, seeing to what depths his companion had fallen. "If it makes any difference to you, I'm sorry I came at you like that. It seems rather silly, thinking about it now. I would so much rather lie here and rest."

"Do you mean it?" asked Hossososo, quieting his sobs with difficulty.

"Certainly," yawned Hipuptup.

"Well in that case," said Hossososo, taking command again of his quavering voice, "I'm sorry that I ran you through. It was a lousy thing to do, and I regret doing it."

"Think nothing of it," said Hipuptup, rousing himself somewhat to do so. "I would have done the same, were I in your position."

"You know who's really to blame," said Hossososo, rising up on his good elbow. "The King is really to blame, for all of it. Who sent us out here on this ridiculous quest? He should have known better. It's simple human nature. A group this large will always fall to fighting amongst itself. Don't you think?"

There was no reply. It seemed to Hossososo that Hipuptup was right, that their discussion could be more eloquently resolved after a night's rest. He closed his eyes, feeling as though there was something more he wanted to say. He just could not think of what it was. He assured himself that he would remember it in the morning. The last thing he thought of before sleep took him was the strange and strangely humorous sound the axe had made, when it was pulled from his body. He let out one final giggle, but then remembered his companion. He did not want to disturb Hipuptup. So instead he lay still, and waited for sleep to come.

6.
The Dead and Wounded

Following the warriors' departure, the remaining enlisted men set about retrieving the bodies of those killed and wounded by the drawbridge mechanism's failure. This proved a great and difficult task, as many bodies had been broken asunder, and many others had been carried to the bottom of the moat by armor and weaponry, and could not be retrieved. Those that could be recovered, wounded and dead alike, were placed in a great pile within the courtyard, where their intermingled moans and cries lingered for two days while the Doctor made his rounds among them, applying a variety of cryptic and ineffective treatments.

"But shouldn't we separate them?" asked the Royal Page, who had been drafted into service as the Doctor's Assistant. "Which is only to say," he went on, reading in the Doctor's silence a hint of annoyance, "that we waste a great deal of time attending to men who a second, closer glance reveals to be deceased. If we were to separate the dead from the wounded..."

"Nonsense!" interrupted the Doctor, turning suddenly about to face the Page. "How else will we motivate the unwell to become well, if not by making them aware in the clearest of all possible terms what exactly is at stake?"

"But the corpses are becoming rather rank," insisted the Page, pulling a face. "Surely it is not conducive to the healing faculties to lie amongst such fetor!"

"My child," replied the Doctor, in a tone expressive of his absolute weariness with the conversation, "I am a *Doctor*. No one in the entire Kingdom knows better than I what is and what is not conducive to the healing faculties. Your task, may I remind you, is to do as *I say*, not to offer your uninformed opinions on subjects of which you have no understanding. Your insistence is not only tiresome, but also detrimental to our purpose. If, however, you maintain that you have something to offer, then allow me to present you with a small test. Take, for example, this man here," and here he indicated the soldier at their feet, a ghostly-white young man bearing a large and still-bleeding gash in his side. "What, pray tell, would you have me do with a case such as this?"

"Well," began the boy, looking uncertainly from the soldier to the Doctor, and back to the solider, "I should think the first thing to do would be to clean the wound. Then, naturally, the bleeding should be stopped, and the site covered over with some clean bandage so that nothing foul might corrupt it."

"Ah ha!" cried the Doctor, in triumph. "You see? You could not be more mistaken. No, the proper course, and you would know if you knew anything at all about medicine, is to look past the obvious problem to the root cause of the disease. In this case, the young man is obviously losing blood at an alarming rate. The only solution, therefore, is to replace the blood he has lost, and thus preserve him long enough for the true cure, which is of course the miracle of the body's own faculties. Therefore, go and fetch me a tankard of sheep's blood, and see that he drinks it all. If no sheep's blood is available a cow's blood will do, but it has been known to lengthen the recovery process."

The Page, put in his place, hurried off to the butcher's, overwhelmed by all that he did not know and, he feared, would never understand. When he returned the soldier was dead and the Doctor fixed the boy in a withering gaze, as though to suggest that the boy's tardiness was the true and final cause of the patient's death.

"Give me that," said the Doctor, taking the tankard from the boy's hands and dropping it as quickly, so that its contents spilled onto the already bloody flagstones. "Now, the next time I tell you to do something you do it sharpish, before any more lives are lost on your account. Do you understand?"

"Yes, sir," replied the boy, on the very brink of tears, and doing his very best to stand up straight and keep from crying.

"All right," said the Doctor, his demeanor softening somewhat at the sight of the Page's obvious distress. "It's not as bad as all that. He was going to die, anyway. They all are. There isn't much anyone can do for anybody. If any of them pull through it will be a complete surprise to me."

The Doctor's estimation proved correct when, after two days of exposure, hunger, and thirst all who had survived the initial disaster had perished. The great bell in the topmost tower tolled once for each life lost, and the King left his bedchamber and stood on the lowest balcony (still some fifty feet above the courtyard flagstones) and considered the scene with solemn gravity (which, owing to his divine ascendancy, acted as something like a benediction, and the gathered families of the fallen were extremely grateful and relieved that now the beloved and departed would find favor in the eyes of God in Heaven, finding first favor in the eyes of His proxy on earth).

"These men," bellowed the King, "gave their lives for a noble and just cause! Each will be given a seat at my table in the Hereafter. Doctor," he went on, scanning the courtyard with little success for the man, for at that height many of those standing below were indistinguishable from one another, and finally fixing him with his gaze only when the Doctor waved, "for your efforts you will be given your weight in gold, and shall be appointed to my Council of Advisors!"

"Your Majesty," said the Doctor, bowing deeply, "I am honored and humbled by your gift."

"Yes, very well," said the King, whose somewhat confused demeanor seemed to suggest that, owing in all probability to the height of the balcony and the lowness of the Doctor's bow, he had failed to hear the Doctor's reply. "Well, yes. Certainly. Very good."

"Highness," said the Doctor, bowing even lower.

At this moment the King unceremoniously quit the balcony, thus indicating the end of the occasion. The Doctor, looking very pleased, rose from his low bow and entered the castle, escorted by the Page. The families of those killed gathered around the pile of corpses, hoping to spot a familiar face or limb. As no list had been compiled of the names or locations of the deceased, no family could be certain whether their beloved departed was indeed among the intermingled bodies, at the bottom of the moat, smashed beyond recognition, or simply and miraculously unharmed and on the road to

Hazaiah's lands. This doubt inclined those present to search without ambition, and it was not long before all but a few had quit the courtyard, leaving behind a great pile of unclaimed bodies.

"But what shall we do with these?" asked one of the remaining enlisted men of another.

"Damned if I know," replied the second. "Wait and hear what the King has to say about it, I suppose."

"I hope He says something soon," answered the first. "They smell something foul. I wouldn't want to deal with them if they smelled any worse."

"That's true enough," agreed the second. And then added, "I should have gone with them. Then, at least, I wouldn't be stuck here wondering what to do with this great mess."

"Nonsense," replied the first. "If you'd gone with them you'd just as likely be *in* that great mess."

"That's true," said the second.

"Further," continued the first, indifferent to the other's agreement, "you know as well as I that you've no business running about the countryside, chopping off the heads of landed lords. The idea of it is laughable."

"I suppose it is," agreed the second.

"The very *idea*," the first repeated, chuckling to himself, "of you! Beating out the others to claim the head of Hazaiah the Terrible! Oh my!" and here he broke down into a fit of uncontrollable mirth, and assumed the entirely indefensible posture of a man about to be sick, bent at the waist with his hands on his knees. In this position, transported as he was, he failed to observe the other who, with scornful expression and reddening face, raised his sword in a menacing and warlike stance and then thrust it to the hilt into the narrow slit between the other's protected shoulder and helmeted head, where a thin crescent of neck remained vulnerable (the other's laughter ceased at once). Limp, the felled man sagged on the blade, and it was only with difficulty (and the proper placement of bracing feet) that the second was able to free his sword. The blade removed, the dead man fell to the flagstones. The second, with a workmanlike air, dragged the body to the pile and hoisted it on top. Then, glancing about to satisfy himself that the courtyard was by now indeed deserted, and he was unobserved, he retrieved his sword and made his exit, wondering vaguely what his wife was making for supper, and whether it was ready yet.

7.
Where Did the King Go?

Where did the King go, when he unceremoniously quit the ceremony? It was a question that no one considered, as every subject already knew of the King's odd and often impulsive behavior. It seemed more than likely that the King simply became bored by the occasion and, finding himself in a position to answer to no one, left. This might have been all that was ever concluded about such a happening (if, indeed, any conclusion was required of so insignificant an event) were it not for the Doctor who, entering the castle, endeavored to find the King with all haste and claim his reward.

"Where is the King? Show me to the King!" he shouted, his voice a pure expression of his triumph.

"Please, sir," answered the Royal Page, following close behind and attempting with difficulty to keep abreast of the Doctor, to whom victory had given wings. "The King is very particular about who He sees, and when He sees them! If the King wishes to see you then you will be seen, but I entreat you not to seek Him out!"

"Where is the King?" the Doctor shouted again regardless, his voice the very soul of self-assurance. "I have business to discuss with Him!" and here he entered the final foyer before the King's bedchamber which, owing to the diminished guard, was occupied only by Hassock, the King's Most Trusted Advisor, who sat on the floor beside the massive and ornately-gilded portal, and whose face bore an expression of absolute exasperation and annoyance.

"Where is the King?" the Doctor demanded again, seemingly oblivious the the Advisor's disposition. And then added, in a gesture of explanation which bespoke, after all, an awareness of his own tactless and intrusive manner, "I've just been awarded a great prize."

"How wonderful for you," replied Hassock, picking dejectedly at the soles of his shoes. "I remember when I was awarded a great prize. That was a wonderful day! The King came to me and said, 'Hassock, for your service to the Kingdom you will be given your weight in gold, and a seat in my Cabinet of Advisors!' I recall it very clearly; I thought my heart would burst with happiness! My mother wept when she heard the news, and my father dared not speak lest he, too, should be overcome with emotion. What a day that was! And now: look what it's all come to!" He hung his head and did not move for several moments, apparently immobilized by his despair.

"Come along," said the Doctor to the Page, when it became clear that Hassock did not intend to continue.

"I really must insist," replied the Page, following nonetheless as the Doctor pushed open the bejeweled doors and entered into the King's private bedchamber.

"Your Majesty!" cried the Doctor.

"Be quiet," replied the King, staring intently at the table before him, upon which lay some dozen grotesque and badly-mutilated forms, and over which hovered a wizened form of indeterminate gender. "Can't you see that I'm busy?"

"I'm terribly sorry, I beg Your Majesty's pardon," replied the Doctor, unbalanced more by the King's cool reception than by the strange scene playing itself out before him. "If Your Majesty would prefer, I could come back at another time and - ,"

"Shush!" cried the King, never taking his eyes from the table.

"You see, you see here!" the other party croaked suddenly. "The way the sparrow's blood pools just so against the hawk's eyeballs! This is a fortunate omen! And the way the lizards' tongues all stick together in a ball like that: well, Your Majesty can understand that I had to show Him right away!"

"Of course, of course," replied the King, the very soul of rapt attention.

"Your Majesty," the Doctor hesitantly offered, "far be it for me to question Your Majesty's decisions! But does the Church not strictly forbid the use of all magics and sorcery, even in the aid of the Crown?"

"Who is this man?" the Conjurer demanded, turning its wrinkled face to the Doctor, who retreated somewhat behind the Page. "How does he ordain to speak to Your Majesty thusly?"

"He is one of my Advisors," the King replied with an indifferent wave, never taking his eyes from the table. "Tell me: what does it mean that the goopy bits are all on one side, and the more solid bits on the other? It certainly seems significant."

"Your Majesty is very perceptive!" replied the Conjurer, returning its attention to the table. "The two distinct and separated masses speak of a coming conflict between two parties, in which one side will find itself wholly overmatched! You see here," it said, extending one surprisingly long and rather meaty finger, "the way the goopy bits all fall to pieces when I shake the table?" and here it shook the table with such violence that much of the offal fell to the floor. "That means that this side will collapse entirely when the battle is joined."

"And how can you be so certain that the goopy bits are the opposing army, and not our own?" replied the King, looking more pleased at having cornered the Conjurer in a clever question than concerned with the answer.

"Why, Your Majesty," interrupted the Doctor, moving rather boldly out from behind the Page. "Surely no army can stand before our own! There can be no question that the goopy bits are our enemies!" and here to show his vehemence he struck at the semi-congealed mass with his fist, spraying a foul-smelling mist over everyone present.

"The Doctor is correct!" the King declared suddenly, and drove his own heavily-bejeweled fist into the goop. "We've nothing to fear: no army can stand before us! At my word ten thousand men will give their lives without a thought!" and here, stomping with mirth, he scattered the table's remaining contents about the floor at their feet.

"Majesty," interrupted the Page. "I know I am only a lowly Page, but I urge Your Majesty to consider more closely our position! Many of the best fighting men in the Kingdom have left its lands on a quest of Your Majesty's own design, and of those that remain I fear very few are up to the task, should our enemies broach our borders. Think of the lives that will be lost! Some preparations must be made, and our soldiers summoned, or I fear we will all suffer for having paid too little heed to the hazards now hanging above our heads!"

A great and anxious silence followed in which Page, Doctor, and Conjurer all watched closely the King's expression, in hopes of divining there some hint of the response to come. The King, considering the draped and ornamented ceiling of his bedchamber, gave a series of long and wet-sounding sighs which, exiting his nostrils, made a slight whistle. Finally, turning his attention to the Page, he placed his hands upon the table and allowed his mouth to hang open for several seconds in an odd and vaguely animal-like expression before he spoke.

"What is your name?" he asked.

"Hypup," replied the Page.

"Uh-huh," said the King. "And your father's name?"

"Hypup, too," said the Page. "I mean he's also Hypup."

"I see," said the King. "And your mother?"

"Hriadi," said the Page, hiding his apprehension and confusion less effectively with each question. "Majesty, I don't understand what -,"

"Shhh," said the King, staring again at the ceiling. Then, with a great burst of breath from his Royal lungs he cried, "Guard! Guard, come in here at once!"

A somewhat uncomfortable silence followed, after which appeared not the guard but rather Hassock, the King's Most Trusted Advisor, looking like he would rather be anywhere else.

"Yes, Majesty?" said Hassock.

"Where is the guard?" asked the King.

"He left with all the others," said Hassock, "as did the guard who is supposed to spell him."

"Ridiculous!" cried the King.   "Who gave them leave to leave?"

"Your Majesty," Hassock began, his voice the very soul of practiced patience, "I told You at the time of Your decree that such problems would invariably arise when so generous a prize was offered so democratically. If You like, I can draft a notice to be carried by messenger to the men on the trail, and ask them to return.   Under the circumstances, I think it would be wise - ,"

"Quiet," said the King, waving his hands at the counselor in frantic annoyance.   "Quiet, quiet, quiet!" Then, drawing himself once again up to his full and dignified height, he said, "Hassock, this boy is guilty of the most egregious pride, and did willfully give voice to seditious and traitorous thoughts! I therefore command you to collect him and his family and lock them away in the lowest dungeon, far from the sight of any loyal citizen, where their subversive agenda can find no welcoming ear!"

"Your Majesty!" cried the Doctor, sufficiently moved to voice, even in his tentative and newly-received role, his objection.

"You cannot!" cried the Page, who burst immediately into tears at the thought of his mother and father suffering so unjustly, and on his account (Hassock, the Most Trusted Advisor, merely shook his head and took the Page by the arm, knowing as the others did not how pointless it was to argue with the King).

"It'll be all right," he said to the Page, once they were out in the hall, and the Page's tears had subsided sufficiently for the Advisor's voice to the heard.   "The dungeon really isn't as bad as it sounds, and anyway I hear that most of the guards have gone off to try their luck claiming Hazaiah's head, and it's gotten very easy to escape. And even if you don't, I doubt very much that the Kingdom will last very long, keeping up the way it has been, and you may be freed before you know it."

"But my parents," the Page blubbered, "how can they ever forgive me for getting them into this pickle? They sacrificed all that they had to get me into Page school, and it nearly cost them their last shekel keeping me in books and uniforms! I'll die from the shame!"

"There, there," replied Hassock, who wasn't really listening, but was considering the worrisome pile of corpses plainly visible in the courtyard below. "You'll see that everything will work itself out. And even if it doesn't, there's no use getting upset about it. Remember that you are a subject first and a citizen second, and everything else will make a little bit more sense. Now: down you go."

They had arrived at the top of a long and dimly-lit stone staircase. Here Hassock remained, while the Page ventured on alone.

Soon the Page was descending in total darkness. Presently he came to a juncture in the narrow corridor: another passageway joined the first, and brought with it a draft of cool air. Having traveled this far in near-frantic apprehension, this cool draft was like the soothing breath of some powerful and beneficent entity: some force beyond human comprehension whispering to Hypup that all was well, that he had nothing to fear. He turned down this second path and stepped almost immediately into nothingness: there was no floor beneath him and he was falling. He had barely enough time to cry out before the ground abruptly arrived and left his impacted and clenching lungs gasping for breath.

"Looks like we've got another one," said the guard, rising to peer in at the prisoner. "This one's just a child. Wonder what he's done, then."

"No telling," replied the other, emerging from the shadows into the light of the various torches positioned at intervals about the room. "Shame we can't ask them. It would be so much simpler if we could trust them to tell the truth."

"Stupidest thing you've ever said," returned the first. "If they were trustworthy they wouldn't be criminals, would they?"

"I suppose not," agreed the second.

"I'm not a criminal," Hypup protested weakly, still unable to fully or artfully manipulate the mechanics of respiration. "I only suggested - ,"

"Shut up in there," said the first guard, swinging a large and nasty-looking club at the bars and causing a terrific clatter which rang in the prisoner's already ringing ears. "Not one more word out of you, or I'll come in there and shut you up myself." Then, turning his attention to the other, he continued: "Really the only thing you can do is wait and see if word comes from above. Usually it does, but sometimes it doesn't. Or, once in a great while, a prisoner will talk in his sleep, and you can figure out from what he says what it is that he's done."

"There certainly is a lot to learn about this job," said the other.

"You just stick by me," replied the first. "I'll teach you everything I know."

Concluding that his efforts would go unrewarded or, very likely, punished, and finding also the monumental effort that these efforts, owing to his injuries, now required, Hypup decided to let the matter drop. He moved to the farthest corner of his cell and considered the emptiness above him, somewhere in which lay the entrance to the second corridor and the edge over which he had unsuspectingly stepped. He wondered if he would be able to climb the walls and thus attempt some escape, and tried to determine just how far he had fallen. But he soon abandoned this effort: there seemed no telling how great the distance might be, and with only opaque darkness above and in his miserable and desperate circumstances the distance seemed insurmountable, whatever its true dimensions.

Finding himself thus undeniably a prisoner, he hung his head and wept. The guards beyond the bars continued their conversation. In the bedchamber above, the King kicked at the offal on the carpet and demanded to know where Hassock had been. Hassock explained that he had escorted the prisoner to the dungeon, and then returned straightaway. He could tell by the King's expression that the King had no idea what he was talking about.

8.
While Back on the Trail...

Back on the trail, the horde had crossed the valley (losing a half-dozen of its members in the process, of which one had been rather old and likely to die even before the trek began, and of which three had been drowned together when the bridge crossing the river at the valley's lowest point collapsed, and just as well could have been one, and of which the remaining two had mortally wounded each other in an argument over a bolt of sackcloth, and who, everyone agreed, while alive had been only a hinderance to the group's forward progress) and entered the Great Forest. Once inside the forest, however, the assembly quickly became lost, as the sun and stars were entirely obscured by the heavy canopy above. Night was nearly indistinguishable from day, and the treetops so high that any scout who climbed up for a better view found that his words vanished in the great distance between himself and the congregation below, and that any sense of direction was lost in the long and circuitous climb down. Nor could they leave the forest for, having become so completely turned around, they could not be certain from which direction they had come.

"We'll die in here, and never reach the other side!" said some of the peasants, many of whom were not brave. "We'll never again see our beloved home!"

"Nonsense," replied other peasants, some of whom were brave and some of whom were only acting brave in the presence of the warriors, in an attempt to impress them. "We'll get out of this, sure enough! And in no time you'll be back at your hearth with your wife at your side, laughing that you ever had a doubt!"

"Quiet, all of you," said Hunhungaroo who, bearing his great axe, was still in charge. "The forest wishes to tell me its secrets, and you drown it out with your prattle. Be silent, or I'll see to it that you are tied to one of these trees and left for whatever horrors lurk in these shadows."

"Who ever heard of such a thing," said one of the peasants to another. "The forest telling him its secrets! He's gone loopy, there's no doubt in my mind."

"Still," replied the other, to whom he was speaking, "I'd rather follow him than wander around here alone."

"That's true enough," agreed the first, hurrying slightly to walk closer behind the man walking in front of him, and treading rather gracelessly on the man's heels. "I'd do just about anything to avoid being left out here alone. My grandfather used to tell me stories about this place when I was just a boy."

"Mine, too," said the second. "He used to tell me a great beast lived in the forest, with a tongue like a great spiked war club and eyes that could freeze you in your tracks, if you looked into them."

"No, that's not it at all," said the first. "The eyes don't freeze you, they turn you into jelly right on the spot. All that's left of you is a puddle and a pile of empty clothes."

"Are you calling my grandfather a liar?" asked the second, stopping suddenly and shoving the first so unexpectedly that the first stumbled off the trail and tripped over a branch. "No one calls my grandfather a liar! I will have you know that he fought to defend the Kingdom in seventeen wars - twelve for the old King and five for his son - and his word is above reproach!"

The first peasant, righting himself, strode back onto the trail and struck the second in the forehead with a pointed rock which he had held, on his approach, in such a way that it would not be seen. The second peasant, bleeding from the wound with a rapidity and volume which surprised everyone, collapsed to the ground and fell into a series of violent convulsions, at the conclusion of which he lay still.

"To hell with your grandfather!" said the first peasant, spitting on the body.

"What's going on here?" said Hunhungaroo, who the commotion had summoned and who was met, upon his arrival, by the nearly frantic peasant and his rock, both of which fell upon the warrior with an unprecedented and startling fury. "Stop it!" shouted Hunhungaroo, shielding himself somewhat ineffectively with the large and, truth be told, somewhat burdensome axe. "I command you to stop this at once!"

The peasant, undeterred by these demands, continued to rain down blows for several moments before those nearby, rousing themselves from shock's torpor, came to the felled warrior's aide. Together they succeeded in removing both the peasant from Hunhungaroo and the rock from the peasant's hands. Hunhungaroo rose somewhat unsteady to his feet and, pressing one gauntleted hand to the substantial gash in his scalp, gave the peasant a savage kick in his protruding belly. The peasant, collapsing to his knees, vomited rather abundantly for one who had, in the last few days, eaten so little.

"It's all your fault," the peasant cried, when his vomiting had subsided. "We'll all die in here, and it will be your fault for bringing us in without the slightest notion of how to get us out again."

"Nonsense," replied Hunhungaroo, still bleeding a great deal but recovering his balance somewhat. "We all entered the forest together. There's no other way to get to Hazaiah's lands! And besides: no one told you to come along. You're here of your own volition."

"I suppose that's true enough," agreed the peasant, furtively searching the ground before him for any rock or stick with which he might assault his warders. "I merely mean to say, that is I only wish to say, and you may correct me if I'm mistaken in my assessment - ," and here, seizing upon a felled and club-like branch, he gave off his rambling and sprang once again to his feet, swinging wildly and indifferently in every direction.

"Stop him, for God's sake!" cried Hunhungaroo, diving backwards and striking his ribs, rather painfully, on a protruding root. "For the love of mercy!"

This melee was brought to a satisfying conclusion when another of the peasants, seizing his opportunity, struck the rampaging man with sufficient force as to render him completely senseless. Tying the offending party to a tree the congregation moved onward, making sure to speak loudly enough to both drown out any cries from the stranded man and convince him absolutely of their irrevocable abandonment.

9.

*During this Rumpus, the Peasants Continued To
Make Their Allegiances...*

During this rumpus the other peasants, undeterred, continued to debate and make their allegiances.

"That one will surely win it," said one or the other of the peasants, of one or the other of the assembled warriors. "Look at those shoulders! Or the way he carries his spear! Or the greatness of his stride! Or his fierce visage! Surely none can stand before one such as him!"

To which another would reply, "Poppycock!"

10.
... While Back in the Village, Questions Were Asked.

While back in the village, the sudden absence of many of the men - soldier and peasant alike - produced many questions which could not be answered by any to whom they were posed. What was so important, they asked, about the head of Hazaiah the Terrible? What would be gained by its receipt? What would be hazarded by allowing it to remain atop the body to which it was presently affixed? Why now, after all, when it was widely rumored and generally believed that foreign armies were advancing at the Kingdom's borders? Under what circumstances would the King compel His citizenry to turn their rude weapons inward upon a *domestic* target, when such obvious intervention was required elsewhere? And even if no such threat existed, why Hazaiah? Why him, when there were certainly many others more reprehensible, traitorous, dangerous? What, exactly, was in the King's mind?

To these and similar questions it was commonly answered that the King was merely out of touch: that his long tenure ensconced within the many and various comforts afforded Royalty had warped his mind, allowing him to harbor such arrogance as was seemingly required of one who would so flagrantly turn his back to his enemy.

"Surely," proponents of this explanation would say, "He has simply spent too much time basking in His own self-glory, and now feels Himself too great to be overcome by any enemy!"

"Not so!" replied others, who went on to posit their own, equally groundless explanation: that Hazaiah was in fact aiding the enemy in their attempts to cross the Kingdom's border undeterred and undetected; that it was only with Hazaiah's collusion that the enemy had any hope of victory; that an example had to be made to show the passively dissident the wages of seditious acts; that, in short, the King knew exactly what he was doing, and that it was not for the peasantry to question his mandates. After all: hadn't the King risen to the Crown by the decree of God Himself?

"We must not question the King!" these loyal citizens cried.

To which the more cynical replied: "Balderdash!"

11.
The More Troubling Question, Undercutting the First

The more troubling question, undercutting the first question, posed by very few (as the implication carried in the question amounted to high treason) was: Why would Hazaiah attack the Kingdom? Did he, as the rumors insisted, delight merely in acts of insurgency? Did he harbor some hateful grudge against the King? Was he generally no good? And, if no reason could be found, was it then more likely that Hazaiah had not attacked the Kingdom? And, if it was indeed more likely that he had not attacked the Kingdom, then for what reason was he accused? For what reason was he slandered to the point of condemnation, and a verdict rendered on the subject by the Crown? To what sinister end was the truth obscured?

This question, dangerous to any who voiced it, was likewise relegated to havens of discreet conversation and thus offered only to sympathetic ears. Having no dissenting position around which it might become anchored, the question gave birth to wild and improbable explanations whose lightest word would have withered under the scrutiny of more public discourse. Most belonged to a theme: that the call for Hazaiah's head was part of an elaborate plot to distract the public from some other, more insidious threat; that the call in fact comprised the central and critical hub of a conspiracy whose exact extent could only be guessed.

"The King is certainly up to something," proponents of this theory agreed.

To which their husbands, wives, sons, daughters, friends or parents, moving about their clandestine, hearthside meetings on some chore or another, interrupted their somber council to cry, "Fiddlesticks!"

12.

The Exact Nature of Hazaiah's Crimes

In the end all such conversations amounted to only so much time-wasting, and often quickly devolved into intractable argument, as no facts existed to substantiate any position or declare the authority of one explanation over another. Though it was generally accepted that Hazaiah was indeed terrible, and responsible for (what everyone felt was likely to be, if an accurate record was ever compiled) innumerable heinous acts, the exact nature of his crimes was not known, as neither trial nor verdict had ever been convened or rendered. Of the crimes for which the King had declared him enemy, it was never unequivocally proven that Hazaiah bore the responsibility for their orchestration: blame had rather been assigned by the convergence and consensus of rumor, accusation, and insinuation, and whatever truths lay hidden within these was, if not lost, at least largely obscured by the scurrilous stance in which they were housed and from which they were delivered.

The facts of the case were the soul of simplicity: several casks of black powder, transported by mule cart, were exploded on three separate occasions in three of the Kingdom's crowded markets, causing numerous deaths and untold injury, and nearly unendurable damage to property and merchandise. On each occasion the driver of the cart, who was responsible for lighting the fuse, had been blown to smithereens (as had his cart and mules) and so no identification could be made nor any connection established between the attack's director and actor (nor could it be established what effect, beyond utter devastation and havoc, the attack was intended to produce: no one of any importance was killed, nor was anyone of any importance likely to be in the area at the time of the attacks).

The Captain of the Guard, casting about in his search for any clue, and nearly frantic in his efforts to allay the public's growing doubt in his abilities, seized upon and mercilessly questioned the man who had sold one of the carts and who, after several days of torture, shouted Hazaiah's name shortly before expiring. But this, too, was the subject of some debate, as several present felt that this cart merchant, sensing the nearness of death, had rather exalted God and exclaimed "Hosanna!" and not the name of the vassal lord. Others present during the inquisition pointed out that rumors of Hazaiah's guilt (perpetuated by an unknown party) predated the merchant's accusation, and that these rumors had in fact been discussed in the merchant's presence during the course of his imprisonment, and that this in itself cast doubt on the information the merchant had provided.

These detractors' positions had, however, little effect on the Captain of the Guard, who with all haste made public the knowledge that Hazaiah had been named.

This sudden break in the case, arriving after weeks of fear and uncertainty, kindled amongst the prejudice and suspicion already at work in the populace and gave birth to innumerable insights and explanations which, fueled (and seemingly validated) by the grief and anger of those professing them, soon comprised the whole of the public discourse on the subject: Hazaiah, it was said by some, was close friends with the previous King, and was exiled from his position of courtly leisure by the current King, for reasons ranging from political disagreement to economic necessity; others explanations claimed that Hazaiah was once an enemy warlord, until his lands were seized by the expanding Empire, making him an unwilling vassal prone to acts of insurgency; no, still others accounts proclaimed: Hazaiah was once a gentle soul, and loved by all, until by misadventure and unfortunate circumstance his heart was possessed by a vile demon (or, in some tellings: until he was cursed by a witch).

Still others explained that it was impossible to know why Hazaiah orchestrated his attacks: that some men were merely evil, that Hazaiah was one of these. This last explanation, being the least specific, was likewise the least burdened by any need for substantiation, and was accordingly the most readily accepted and most widely disseminated (and, being a question of nature rather than deeds, leant as much veracity to the other explanations as it derived from them in an exchange whose baseless and circular logic nevertheless seemed to encompass all of the facts and rule out all other possibilities, until Hazaiah's guilt seemed incontrovertible and beyond debate).

13.
The Page's Family

"But what's this all about?" the Page's father asked of the Captain of the Guard, who now stood in the family's doorway. "My son works in the Castle, it's true, but that has little to do with my wife and me! Honestly, I've no idea why the Captain of the Guard should find it necessary to call upon us."

"Unless something has happened to our son," replied the Page's mother, a note of concern entering her voice. "Even still, I doubt very much that the Captain of the Guard would be sent to deliver the news. I have heard that many have left the Kingdom, but still I cannot believe that no one less important could be found to deliver whatever news it is you have to deliver."

"Your son has been taken prisoner," replied the Captain of the Guard who, truth be known, had only been appointed Captain of the Guard that morning, as the old Captain of the Guard could not be found, being, it was assumed, either on the quest for Hazaiah's head, at the bottom of the moat, or piled in the courtyard. "I'm afraid I'll have to ask you to accompany me. There are several matters pertaining to his imprisonment that require your attention."

"Great God deliver us!" cried the Page's mother, and collapsed in her grief and could not be moved.

"There, there," said her husband, kneeling beside her and patting her, reassuringly, on the shoulder. "I'm sure it will all be resolved shortly, if we merely follow along with what the Captain asks of us. I'm sure it's all just a misunderstanding that will be easily resolved when all the facts are brought to light," and here he looked, for accord, to the Captain of the Guard.

"Hard to say," replied the Captain of the Guard, whose previous post had not prepared him for these delicate situations. "I suppose anything is possible, but still if I were you I might prepare myself for the worst, just to be on the safe side."

At this the Page's mother let out a prolonged wail which seemed to extend beyond the limits of human ability and which convinced the Captain of the Guard, momentarily, that some supernatural and unholy force was at work. Springing into action he struck the Page's mother on the back of the head (which, owing to the angle at which she lay, was entirely exposed to such an assault), rendering her instantly senseless and ending effectively her prolonged and stentorian expression of grief.

"What?" cried the Page's father, in shock and surprise, rising instantly to his feet. "How? Why? What is the meaning - ? How could you - ? I'll have your - ! Why I should - !"

"Sir," replied the Captain of the Guard, brandishing the stick with which the offending blow had been delivered, "I would recommend that you calm yourself! There's no need to become excited or agitated. A small matter arose which required intervention, but it's over now. Your wife was clearly attempting to work some sort of magic or charm, but the threat has been neutralized."

"My wife was - ? You think that - ?" said the Page's father, too upset to complete a thought.

"Men!" called the Captain of the Guard, summoning the six other guardsmen who stood outside, "we'll have these two into the Castle. This is by special request of the King Himself, so let's do it sharpish. I don't want to take all day at it, anyway. Like to get home to show the wife the new uniform. I told her as I was leaving this morning that today was going to be my day. I couldn't have told you why I felt - ."

His speech was here unexpectedly halted by the sudden application of the Page's father's hands to his unprotected throat. The other guardsmen, witnessing the scene, and attempting to enter and aid their Captain, found instead that their way was blocked by the Captain of the Guard himself who, locked in conflict with the Page's father, filled the small doorway. Instead, gathering in a cluster outside, these guardsmen attempted alternately to push their way inside and to pull the Captain out by force, both of which efforts failed due to their uncoordinated timing, as some were pushing as others were pulling; during these farcical attempts the Captain's face grew redder and redder, and soon began to turn an unhealthy-looking shade of bluish-purple, which anyone in the Kingdom would have recognized at that time as being if not identical to then at least reminiscent of the unnatural hue exhibited by the numerous corpses piled in the Castle's courtyard.

This scene concluded suddenly when, following a pronounced cracking sound (plainly audible even over the shouting of the guardsmen and the clanking of their armor), the Captain of the Guard emitted an unnatural gurgling sound and went suddenly limp. His body, held aloft by the various parties attempting to move it, remained artificially upright. Seizing upon this opportunity one of the guardsmen, his spear lowered, ran at full speed into the doorway, impaling murdered and murderer alike so that, the spear relinquished to its recipients, the two fell chest-to-chest upon the floor. The Page's mother, reclaiming slowly her faculties, screamed at the sight and fell instantly to attacking with her fists and nails the nearest of the guardsmen who, unsheathing his sword, felled her with such ease that the effect was unexpectedly comic, and all of the guardsmen laughed.

"I suppose there's nothing more for us here," said one of them, after they'd all had a good chuckle. "Three more for the pile, then. You two take up the ends of that spear, and see if you can't carry them that way. I'll take the wife." He lifted the woman's corpse with ease and placed it across his shoulders. Then they left, bearing the dead amongst them.

But when they reached the courtyard, they were informed by the guard standing watch that no more corpses were to be added to the pile.

"What do we do with them now?" asked the guardsman carrying the back of the spear, when they were back outside the Castle gates.

"We should have just left them," said the guardsman carrying the front of the spear, considering the blisters forming on his palms.

"I know what we'll do," said the guardsman carrying the Page's mother.

Four of the guardsmen took hold of the spear, while two held the Page's mother upright. Then the four ran at the two, impaling the Page's mother as well. Bearing the sagging spear between them the guardsmen moved to the moat's edge where, with a great swinging heave, they were able to throw the spear and its contents some little distance across the water. It struck the surface with a great splash and, weighed down by the Captain of the Guard's armor, quickly sank.

The guardsmen, their anxieties allayed by the problem's tidy resolution, laughed when, reentering through the Castle gate, the watchman considered them with obvious and comic confusion, and inquired after their burden's destination, to which inquiry he received in reply only their unchecked and raucous chortling.

14.
While High Above, the King

While high above, the King was troubled in his napping by frightful and unnatural dreams. An eagle flew with a worm in its talons; a feast table was overturned; a great dog stood barking at the window; a mountain on the horizon refused to stay still. He awoke in terror and called for the Soothsayer, who reassured him that all were, though frightening to the untrained mind, pleasant omens predicting prosperity and success to the King in all of his endeavors. Didn't the King's family crest, after all, bear the image of the eagle? And what could an overturned feast table mean, but that the King had such plenty that he might overturn a table without hesitation?

Reassured, the King returned to his bed. He dreamed that a cat with eight legs had entered his bedchamber, and climbed upon his face. Finding that he could not breathe, the King awoke with a start and looked about the bedchamber for an eight-legged cat. He soon abandoned his search. He wondered what the Soothsayer would have to say about this dream. He decided that perhaps he would rather not know.

15.
While Outside, Hassock and the Soothsayer

While outside the King's bedchamber door, Hassock and the Soothsayer were arguing.

"You must not tell Him such things!" cried Hassock. "Please, I beg of you, in the name of every citizen in our Kingdom, in the name of almighty God Himself!"

"I'd like to know what you know about it," said the Soothsayer, with obvious annoyance. "Who are you to tell me of the interpreting of dreams? I received my training under Huffguffgaroo, whose reputation speaks for itself! I am the foremost authority on dreams in this and three neighboring Kingdoms! For sixty years I have traveled the lands, telling Prince and peasant alike the meaning of the visions that trouble their sleep. Now you - ,"

"Yes, yes, I know all of that," replied Hassock, interrupting rather rudely, and glancing nervously at the chamber door, for it seemed that the volume of the Soothsayer's towering indignation might rouse the King, and cause even more problems. "I do not mean to tell you your business! But the King has offered such an extravagant reward for so frivolous a prize that He has effectively reduced the Royal and national armies to a level at which they cannot hope to thwart the efforts of an advancing enemy! It is imperative to us all that the King immediately rescind the call for Hazaiah's head, that He be made to appreciate the tenuous and precarious position in which His Kingdom stands! Such cannot be accomplished when all foreboding dreams and omens are explained away, and the King patted on His back at every turn!"

"If you are so hot to tell the King that He is doing something wrong, then I invite you to do so yourself!" replied the Soothsayer. "My first concern is and will remain my own well-being, and there is no surer way to put that in jeopardy than to give the King bad news! I would think that you, of all people, would know that by now."

"I do, I do," replied Hassock, covering his face with his hands in irrepressible frustration. "But the King has no more regard for me than He has for the carpets upon which He treads! What good is it being the King's Most Trusted Advisor if the King doesn't listen to *any* of His Advisors?"

"Calm yourself," said the Soothsayer, placing a withered and reassuring hand on Hassock's shoulder. "Tell me: what do you dream when you close your eyes at night?"

"I see a great field," replied Hassock, wiping away frustrated tears. "In this field are six cows, each with six horns."

"This is a very good sign," said the Soothsayer. "It means you will have six years of prosperity, and the voices that proclaim your victory will shout with the strength of thirty-six horns."

"Oh," said Hassock.

"You shouldn't worry so much," said the Soothsayer.

"I suppose I could try to worry less," replied Hassock.

"I would recommend it," agreed the Soothsayer, and here produced from within its ponderous robes a vile of pale, yellow-green fluid. "Here: this will help you. Take a small sip of this when you get to feeling nervous. It's Huffguffgaroo's recipe, but I've improved it a bit. If you need more you know where to find me. It's very good. It's the same potion I used to help King Hillgugu the Heartsick overcome his fear and ride into battle."

"King Hillgugu was killed in battle," replied Hassock, taking the vial nonetheless.

"Well there's no accounting for luck," countered the Soothsayer, a little too defensively. "And anyway, fighting isn't my department. If you want your dreams read, you come see me. If you want to learn to fight, you ask a warrior."

"I would," replied Hassock, "if I could only find one!" And here he again broke down, once again overwhelmed by the great disaster looming ever on his mind's horizon.

"Drink up," said the Soothsayer, indicating the vial.

"Thank you," said Hassock, who uncorked the potion and, in a single swallow, emptied the vial of its contents.

"Oh dear," said the Soothsayer. "I did say a sip, after all. You can't blame me for whatever adverse effects you experience. I made it very clear that you were to take no more than a sip when you felt nervous. I can't be held responsible for what people do of their own free will, after all."

"What do you mean?" said Hassock, beginning to feel something strange and not terribly pleasant somewhere in his middle. "What do you mean, adverse effects?"

"Whatever happens," said the Soothsayer, "just remain calm and rest assured that the symptoms will pass in a few hours. Well, perhaps a bit longer in this case. That was an awful lot you drank just now. Hard to say, under such circumstances, when things will happen. Now if you'll excuse me, I really must be running along. I have other clients to see."

"Wait," Hassock weakly protested, as the robed figure retreated down the hall and into the blur now forming at the edges of his vision. "What do you mean, adverse - ? I have several things to do this afternoon, and can't possibly - ."

He was interrupted by the sound of glass shattering somewhere nearby. Looking around he discovered the remnants of the vial scattered about his feet. This filled him with confusion, for he was certain that he still held the vial in his hand. He looked from one to the other, but failed to discover it there. He had the sudden and pressing need to tell someone - someone in charge - to wait, and beg them to explain what was happening to him very clearly and slowly. He was certain that, armed with this explanation, he would be able to artfully negotiate his strange new circumstances. He felt, in his last conscious moments, greatly distraught that no such person could be located.

16.

The Force Massing at the Kingdom's Border

Three hundred miles east of Hazaiah's lands, the enemy's army was massing at the border. Several hundred soldiers (one quarter of which rode on horseback) led a column of catapults, cannons, and fortified towers; behind these followed several hundred more soldiers (nearly half of which rode on horseback) who pulled behind them a number of experimental implements designed to tear down the high wall surrounding the Castle.

"We'll tear down their wall!" shouted the Commander, waving his saber above his head. "We'll tear it down, and make them sorry they ever heard of Isthinrod!"

"For Isthinrod!" resounded the several hundred, beating their breastplates.

"For King Isthisthis!" added a soldier standing somewhere in the group's middle, producing with this offering a volley of shouted rejoinders, and sending the assembled force into a near frenzy.

"Easy men!" shouted the Commander. "Save it for the enemy!"

"For Isthinrod!" repeated the several hundred, in something less than unified voice.

"Kill them all!" shouted a soldier standing somewhere near the front, inciting a thunderous chorus of reiterations and causing an almost complete breakdown in the group's careful formation.

"Back in line, men!" shouted the Commander, excitedly waving his saber.

"For Isthinrod!" shouted one of the soldiers, whose cry was met and matched by nearly everyone in the group, which stopped completely as its members fell to shouting excited encouragements to themselves and one another.

"For pity's sake!" shouted the Commander, compulsively striking his helmet with the flat of his saber, as the entire force came rather gracelessly to a full stop (much of the equipment was too heavy to be stopped so abruptly, and several servicemen were injured and one crushed beneath the wheels of the catapult before these implements could be successfully brought under control; several other servicemen were injured when, oblivious to the disturbance ahead and distracted by something or other, they marched into the rears of horses stopped in front of them and were unceremoniously kicked).

"For Isthinrod!" cried many of the several hundred, as yet oblivious to the disaster.

"Ooooh!" cried the wounded, grabbing unproductively at their injuries.

"Great gravy!" cried the Commander, seeing what disaster and injury this breakdown in forward progress had wrought, and still compulsively slapping the flat of his saber against his helmet. "We'll have to camp here tonight, and see to the wounded! We'll lose two days at least! Oh this is a disaster, an absolute disaster!"

17.
The Reason for the Invasion

The camp being established, the men fell to talking amongst themselves.

"What do you suppose their army is like?" asked one soldier of the others. "I've heard that it's vast beyond compare, that their wall has never been breached in all of the centuries that the Castle has stood. I hear that their men do not fear death, and that their women will seduce you and then murder you while you slumber."

"I heard something similar," agreed another. "I heard also that they send their children into enemy camps dressed as urchins selling pies, but that the pies are made from the corpses of their felled enemies: are made, in fact, from the encamped men's fallen brethren. They're vicious monsters, every one of them."

"Nonsense," replied a third, who was a good deal older than the others, and more experienced in battle. "They're men, same as you or I. They bleed and can be killed. There's nothing more that needs to be said. And as for their wall, we'll have it down in no time. A wall, like a man, is put together bit by bit, and can be taken apart just the same."

"I'm surprised to hear you speak so assuredly about the wall," said another soldier, speaking up. "I heard a rumor that the entire reason for the attack was to test out the new equipment and see if it is able to bring down a wall such as the one we plan to assault."

"That's absurd," replied the third, older and more experienced than the others.

"Yes," agreed the first, "surely Good King Isthisthis wouldn't send us to fight and possibly be killed for something so trivial!"

"It's hardly trivial," replied the fourth. "After all, we're not crawling about in the mud anymore. You should see what sort of walls kings are building these days! I've travelled as far as the Farfish Sea, and along my journey witnessed walls you would think men incapable of erecting. Massive walls two dozen yards thick, with integrated portcullises and caches of black powder large enough to blow any assaulting force to smithereens! Believe me when I tell you: the wall and the ability to effectively destroy it is the key to modern warfare."

"It's still absurd," replied the third, a note of annoyance entering his voice. "I didn't march out here to see if the King's new toy works or not! Whatever the King's reason for sending us out, I'm certain it's a perfectly good one! Moreover, I'm certain that it isn't for the reason that you're saying it is."

"He certainly seems to know something about it," said the second of the fourth to the third, prompting the third to scoff and storm off.

"I wonder what's eating him?" said the first, when the third was gone.

"What difference does it make anyway?" said the fourth, moving closer in to the others and beginning to warm his hands at their fire. "He's grown old and slow and grumpy, and likely won't survive the assault. So forget him!"

He laughed, and the other two exchanged concerned glances.

"But sir," offered the first, "doesn't the thought that our countryman will not survive the attack trouble you in the least?"

"Why should it?" replied the third, helping himself to what was bubbling in the two's cook-pot. "I've been around enough to know the one unimpeachable truth of life: every man looks out for himself!" He laughed again. "Take, for example, this assault. I know that the King is looking out for Himself when He studies the mechanics of wall demolition. He, Himself, hides behind a wall! Knowing that the King is looking out for Himself and only Himself, I have no qualms about looking out for myself. You see? It's very simple!" He took another large ladleful and then began flapping his hands at his face, fanning the steaming mouthful with a look of profound discomfort. This, however, seemed to prove ineffective, and in another second he was on his feet and running off in the direction of the stream on the banks of which the camp had been made.

"What do you think?" asked the first of the second, when the fourth was gone.

"I don't know," replied the second. "He certainly did sound like he knew what he was talking about."

"True," agreed the first. "But then: so did the other, before he stormed off."

"You're right," agreed the second.

"I suppose it doesn't matter, anyway," said the first, a note of melancholy entering his voice. "After all: we're here, aren't we? And it's not as if we're going to run off, whatever the reason is for the attack."

"No," agreed the second, "I suppose we're not going to do that." And then added, "At least not until we know for sure."

"Right," said the first, "not until we know for sure."

Beside the stream, the fourth soldier knelt and splashed water onto his burning tongue. Rising, he inadvertently bumped into the haunch of a horse that was munching the grass beside him. The horse reflexively kicked, striking the soldier in the back of the head and sending him sprawling, facedown, into the stream.

For a moment a long string of bubbles rose and broke on the surface, gently disturbing the fan of hair that floated around the soldier's head. The horse, turning about to face its assailant, considered these bubbles with some fascination. Then the bubbles unexpectedly ceased. The man's body began to gyrate and spasm as his brain, denied the oxygen it craved, sent meaningless signals through the matrix of nerves that ran throughout his body. All of this was to no avail, as the man had been knocked senseless by the horse's kick. He was no more aware of his brain's final desperate attempts than he was of the stream in which he lay, the field through which it cut, the encampment nearby, or the horse who stood watching him with rapt, ignorant curiosity.

18.

The Peasant Who Was Left in the Woods

The peasant who, subsequent to his attack on Hunhungaroo, was bludgeoned into unconsciousness and abandoned by the horde, awoke some time later to discover: firstly, that he was bound rather tightly to the tree against which he stood; secondly, that the congregation of warriors and attendant peasants was nowhere in the area; and thirdly, that there was a small and rather aged man standing before him, studying him with what seemed to be great interest and curiosity. This man wore no clothes, but his beard had grown to such lengths that he was able to wear it wrapped about his middle, in a manner sufficient to preserve his modesty. His ribs protruded startlingly from his sunken belly and his bulging eyes stared from the recesses into which they had retreated. The hair on his head stood in a great tangle or fell in matted locks which swung ponderously as he made small, furtive movements, seemingly considering the peasant from many angles. In all he had the look of one who had lived outside of society and its habits for many years.

"What are you looking at?" demanded the peasant, attempting rather unsuccessfully to move farther around the tree to which he was bound.

The other, considering the peasant with unwavering interest, repeated the question a number of times in a voice which, if it could be said to resemble anything, resembled perhaps the sound of a waterwheel squeaking and groaning as it made its way around.

"All right, that's enough of that," said the peasant, attempting once again some retreat as the other came closer. "You can see I'm in bad shape as it is; you needn't add to my sorrows with your mockery."

"Bad enough shape, bad enough shape as it is!" cried the other in triumph. "Bad enough shape as it is, needn't mock me, what are you looking at? Bad enough, bad enough!" and here he fell to executing a frantic sort of dance, jumping and crouching and running in circles in a display of what seemed to be irrepressible excitement and enthusiasm.

"Stop that!" cried the peasant, craning his neck to follow the strange man with his eyes. "Please, for the love of God, you must stop at once! I'll go mad if you don't!"

"Mad if you don't, mad if you don't!" repeated the other in a sing-song voice.

The peasant, finding himself powerless to alter his situation, blinked back frustrated tears. He wished, wholeheartedly, that he had never left his home, nor heard of the King's call for Hazaiah's head. He recalled, with stunning clarity, the morning upon which he had departed, and the fact that he could not re-enter and alter that moment (which, in his mind, seemed so very near) startled, horrified, and infuriated him. He closed his eyes and prayed with all his soul for God to intervene and enact some miraculous transformation by which he would be transported back to his home and that moment in time. He thought he heard, for an instant, his wife's voice from the other room, and his children's laughter. He opened his eyes and discovered that no miracle had been performed: that he was bound in time's ambivalent forward progress as inexorably as he was bound to the tree at his back.

He felt certain that he would die: that the strange man, in his disregard for civilization and its ways, would kill him out of boredom or tragic curiosity; that he would be attacked and eaten by some beast; that he would eventually starve, unable to secure any means of escape. Exhausted by his despair, he hung upon the ropes which bound him. Indifferent to the world beyond his own sorrow he was unaware of the strange man's movements, and so was taken wholly by surprise when the rope binding him gave way. The stranger, dancing about, waved triumphantly the stone knife with which the deed had been accomplished.

"Needn't mock me!" he cried. "Bad enough shape! Bad enough shape as it is!"

The peasant groaned and roused himself with some discomfort, having landed rather heavily and gracelessly upon the unforgiving forest floor. Wiping away the blood that issued from his now swollen and misshapen nose he expressed in a nasal whine his gratitude to the stranger and to God and all of the angels in Heaven above. This task concluded, he fell upon the stranger with terrible ferocity, striking and tearing at exposed flesh and matted hair, until the stranger lay senseless before him. Then, taking the stone knife (which during the scuffle had been thrown clear, and lay some dozen paces away) the peasant set off in great and murderous haste, declaring to the whole of the vast and indifferent forest his oaths and pledges of vengeance.

19.
The Warriors' Progress

Meanwhile, the warriors (and the peasants with them) had become hopelessly lost.

"We're hopelessly lost!" cried the peasants, wringing their hands. "Oh, how we wish we'd never come on this fool's errand! We pray that Almighty God might deliver us from this fate, for surely we will starve, or be killed by some beast, or become lost forever and grow old and too weak to continue!"

"Shut your flapping jaws!" replied the warriors, doing their best to quell their own rising terror. "We've only to keep heading in one direction, and soon enough we'll be out of this blasted forest!"

A number of scouts had been dispatched, but of these several had not returned, and of those that had returned none had seen anything to indicate that the direction in which they had explored was the one leading out of the forest and onto the shores of the Infinite Lake. It was a melancholy time, and many of the peasants felt too depressed even to make their allegiances, finding their energies better spent in the voicing of lamentations which echoed around the company as it marched by day and resonated through its camp at night.

"I wish those blasted peasants would shut their blasted mouths," said Hunhungaroo, poking with obvious annoyance at a chunk of wood that refused to burn. "It's bad enough being stuck in these blasted woods with them, listening to them argue all day, having to smell them all the time. It's quite another to have to listen to this!"

"We wouldn't have to listen to them all the time," said another of the warriors, seated across the campfire, "if you hadn't gotten us so completely and hopelessly lost."

"Quiet yourself, Hafafanot," replied Hunhungaroo, sitting up and speaking in his most authoritative tone. "What would you have me do? Not one of us knows the way!"

"Still," joined a third, "I have to agree with Hafafanot. You have been leading us this whole time, and look where it's gotten us."

There was a murmur of consent from the others seated nearby, while in the sprawl of the camp beyond a half-dozen or so peasants joined their voices in a prolonged and mournful wail whose echo outlasted for several eerie and unsettling seconds the last voice's cessation.

"I defy any man here to do better than I've done," said Hunhungaroo, rising from the log on which he sat and standing at his full height. "If you think you are better suited than I, then stand and lay your claim!" and here he drew with a great flourish his sword and dagger.

"Sit down," said Hafafanot, waving a dismissive hand. "There's no need for drawn blades."

"Stake your claim!" cried Hunhungaroo, brandishing his steel and wholly ignoring Hafafanot. "I challenge any man who would challenge me!"

"Please," said Hafafanot, rising and moving toward Hunhungaroo. "I am much older than you, and know a thing or two that you, in your brief years, have not yet come to learn. I tell you that this quarrel counts for nothing! Would you turn your blade against friend and foe alike? These men here are your allies against troubles greater than any King's quest. Please, I beseech you! Sheath your steel and let us speak with reason and patience, for murder shall never free us from this forest. Here: give unto me," and here he held out his hand. Hunhungaroo, considering the circle of faces about the fire, handed as a gesture of accord the dagger to his older compatriot. Hafafanot received it and, taking it by the handle, drove it to the hilt up into the soft place behind Hunhungaroo's chin. A low moan escaped from the killed man's throat that, were his teeth not clamped together by the deeply-buried blade, might have been a final curse or cry of pain.

The others, seated about the fire, considered the scene with wary ambivalence while in the camp beyond a pair of voices could be heard, mournfully entreating Heaven's mercy.

"Thus to you!" cried Hafafanot, and here removed the dagger with a yank, allowing the lifeless body to collapse like a disused toy. "We've no more use for you or your worthless command!" and, turning about to face the others, he brandished the bloodied dagger above his head in triumph.

"That's all well and good," said the warrior who had previously agreed, "but what will we do now? I don't imagine any of us wants the job of leading this outfit, seeing as what kindly rewards are offered for the service."

"I agree with Hifftiffbariff," said another, speaking up. "I know I don't want the job."

"Me neither," agreed another, and the few others murmured their accord.

"All right," said Hafafanot, resuming both his seat and his previous, level demeanor. "Suppose we elect one of the peasants to lead? That would certainly give them something to do, rather than wailing all the time! And who knows: they might actually find our way out!"

"I rather like that," said Hifftiffbariff. "Yes: and if we end up lost again we'll let the peasants deal with it themselves. No more need for us to fight amongst ourselves, killing each other for the privilege of leading this smelly mob!"

There was further and resounding consent from all others present. Soon three were dispatched from the fire: one to make the rounds to the other warriors, and inform them of the plan, and two to select a suitable peasant each, between which the other peasants might select a leader at daybreak. These three returned, a toast was raised to Hafafanot and his brilliant plan, and several gallons of wine consumed in the general celebratory spirit of the occasion. Later, the small group having become quite drunk, a fight broke out in which one man was killed and two grievously injured. These wounded lay where they fell, and in the morning were still alive enough to witness the election of the peasant leader. The man picked was of portly stature and simple disposition, and declared as his first act that the party should henceforth march single-file. This ridiculous suggestion proved surprisingly effective, as it ensured both that the company maintained its direction and that the peasants, kept in place, could make no further professions of their allegiance. Soon the trees began to thin, and a vibrant shimmer to appear between their trunks of such pure and wondrous light that some became convinced that it was sorcery, and would proceed no further. Those that did continue soon discovered the gleam to be no more than the sun's reflection on the surface of a lake so vast that its far shore was only a hazy phantasm in the distance.

"The Infinite Lake!" cried the peasants. "Hooray, hooray, hooray!" and fell to dancing with delight and shouting their gratitude toward the blue and cloudless heavens. "A miracle! God has delivered us! All praises be!"

"Beginners luck," mumbled the warriors, who even in their annoyance (that the peasant had succeeded where they had failed) could not repress their joy at having been delivered from the seemingly interminable forest.

Camp was made, and fish were caught and cooked, and several dozen more gallons of wine consumed, and it was only in the morning (when the festive spirit was replaced by headaches and vomiting) that the company began to consider the question of how so vast a body of water, in the utter absence of any seafaring vessel, might be overcome.

20.
While Down in the Dungeon...

While down in the dungeon, Hypup the former Page sat upon the filthy stones and moaned and wept for three days and three nights, until finally the pair of guards on duty could stand it no more, and took pity on him, and one said to the other, "Do you suppose we could let the lad out? Just for a bit? He seems unlikely to attempt any escape, and in any event whatever shenanigans he might try can certainly be overcome by our combined efforts."

"I suppose no harm can come of it," said the other, considering the boy (whose eyes were now so taxed by crying that no further tears would come). "He certainly seems a sorrowful lad, and too wrought with despair to make any effort against us."

"True, true," said the first, considering the boy. "Mercy, but it is a thing to see what a toll despair can take on a body!"

Having reached their decision they rose together and, fitting the key into the lock, opened the cell door, all the while making various coaxing entreaties and gestures to show the boy their benevolent intentions. But Hypup, considering them with weary indifference, made no move towards them, nor toward the open doorway only a few feet from him. They persisted nonetheless, cooing and calling, vehemently declaring their abhorrence of everything their imaginations could proffer of which they suspected the boy might suspect them. These, too, came to no avail, and soon the guards retreated in confusion and frustration to consider their charge, and his curious behavior.

"Perhaps he is ill," said the first guard to the second, "and too weak even to crawl!"

"No," said the second, although perhaps more to himself than to his companion. "Certainly he is just overwhelmed by his misfortune, and indifferent to his circumstances, as any of us might be when faced with similar hardships!"

"We'll leave him for now," said the first, "and see if presently he does not rouse himself."

Meanwhile the other prisoners, seeing that the Page's door had been opened, began to call to the guards.

"Pig-nose!" cried one. "Has the world turned over on its ends, the land replaced the sky, Heaven switched places with the earth, so that the keeper of the keys is now the opener of locks? Have horses learned to fly and birds learned to trot? Do men live in fields and cattle house in hovels? What is going on here?"

"Pig-breath!" cried another, urinating as he did through the cell bars into the harrow hallway. "Have you forgotten yourself? Has the King learned mercy?"

"Pig-offal!" cried a third, squatting to defecate upon the stone and earthen floor. "Do you no longer find your work satisfying? Are you in search of another profession? Or has the prison become a boarding house, and you its innkeeper? If so, a flagon of ale for my friends and me!" and here he let forth a great stream of foul-smelling and unhealthy-colored filth, laughing as he did so.

"Scum!" said the first guard, approaching the cell of the last to speak. "Garbage, waste, human filth! Are you all of such odious nature that you would mock even mercy shown a child?"

"I mock mercy as the world mocks mercy!" came the reply. "Do you think it otherwise?"

"You'll not learn the content of my thoughts, cretin," said the guard, striking the cell's bars with a club kept handy for just such shows of strength and assertions of hierarchy.

"Then do not trouble me with your prattling!" replied the prisoner, still without bothering to rise from his crouch. "Your thoughts: I laugh to hear you speak the word! You have no thoughts! Your sentiments are like two moths, chasing each other about the dark and narrow confines of your skull!" and here he let forth a second in what was to be a series of unpleasant expulsions, of such foul sight and smell that the guard turned away in disgust.

"Ridiculous!" said the guard to the other. "He accuses me of ignorance, and yet he squats in his own filth like an animal!" and the two of them laughed in unified disdain and immitigable authority.

"Yes, such is what you have made me!" cried the prisoner in reply, rising suddenly to his feet and approaching the bars with such speed that the guard, turning back, recoiled to the opposite wall as he found himself nearly nose-to-nose with the cell's inhabitant. "Did you know, Pig-brain, that I was once a man of refinement and learning, a highly respected scholar? Did you know, Pig-tongue, that I lived for many years in luxury, in the employ of the Royal Family? Can you imagine, with your dim animal mind, that I was once first amongst the King's council? Look upon me now, and see what horrors might befall a man of status and power!" and here he stooped and, taking his own filth in his hands, began to fling it with great force and fury, befouling the wall opposite.

"Merciful heavens!" cried the guard, who had moved out of the way in the nick of time, and only narrowly avoided the prisoner's salvo. "I might have believed him, but for this!"

"It's true," said the second prisoner, before whose cell the guard now stood. "He once was a great and powerful man. I saw him once, standing beside the King on the highest balcony. The King was just a boy then, and did all that his Advisor advised him to do. Such is the wage of considered council! The boy became a young man, and no longer found use for the wise sage's words."

"Pig-brains!" shouted the former Advisor, "come here! I have something for you!"

"Such might become of any man," added the first prisoner, with a note of solemn reverence for the man that the prisoner had once been. "Imagine being left in darkness and misery for so long. Just imagine! No wife, no friends, no children, no books! Nothing but the same bare walls, the same unyielding bars: what can a man do, but go hopelessly mad?"

"Certainly one might hold onto one's faith in God," replied the second guard, coming to stand beside his colleague, "and so stave off the call to madness."

"You might wish it so!" replied the first prisoner who, not including the young page, had been in the dungeon for the briefest interval, and likewise retained significant vestiges of his former reason. "I know of no man who wishes to believe that all he has worked to make of himself might be so easily and so succinctly wiped away. Alas, the evidence is to the contrary! You of all people should understand what changes may be wrought by such conditions," and here he made a broad gesture with his arms, indicating not only his own cell but the whole of the dungeon beyond, thereby suggesting that, though they remained free men, the guards themselves were certainly not unfamiliar with the matter of his argument, and were no doubt the unhappy recipients of some similar alteration.

"It's true!" wailed the second guard, with such unexpected volume that his companion dropped the club with which he had troubled the bars. "I've remained silent lo these many years, always insisting to my protesting heart that any job is a good job, the state of the world being what it is, and that I should just hold my tongue and do my duty. But at what cost?" and here he burst into a fit of coughing interspersed with unabashed tears.

"Great goodness!" cried his companion, taking his friend by the shoulders. "What ever is the matter with you? Come: come and sit with me, and we will soon discover and purge the source of this sorrow!"

The first leading the second, they exited the narrow passageway and came into the broader space within which sat their station and off of which stood the Page's cell, its door still standing wide.

"Come," repeated the first, draping a comforting arm about his compatriot's shoulders, "tell me! What is it that troubles you so? Certainly you've found nothing so resounding in their chatter that it would unsettle you so profoundly! Is it trouble at home? Are your parents well? Has some private misfortune befallen you, which you have failed to share with me? Come: unburden yourself, and you will soon find that all may be mended!"

"Oh my friend!" cried the second, writhing in obvious agony as the mournful secret now arose within him. "I am lost, I am lost! My faith has deserted me! Sitting in church on a Sunday I find that my thoughts will not hold, that they tarry and wander hither and thither, that they travel every path but that which leads to Almighty God! I bow my head to pray, and yet my mind will not honor the sacred duty with which it has been charged! I admit - to my great sorrow and with a heart full of shame! - that I have here opened my eyes, and been confronted by the serene faces of those seated beside and around me, their thoughts Holy and their souls at peace! And methinks I hear in these moments the Devil's laughter in my ears... Oh I am lost, hopelessly lost!"

"Calm yourself!" commanded the other. "Calm yourself and hear me, and hear with my words the stuff of your salvation! For I assure you heartily that you are not lost: that such trifles count for nothing, that they matter little in Heaven's estimation!"

"Do not mock me with your blasphemies!" cried the second guard, in a voice both desperate and violent. "I know the nature of God's will upon the earth, and tell you that He has made good to absent Himself from my heart for reasons which I cannot fathom, for sins which I cannot discover and so for which I can make no contrition!"

"My friend!" replied the first, in a voice as infused with mirth as his comrade's had been with anger. "There are subtler explanations for these troubles! And even if there were not, I defy you to discover any man whose thoughts do not wander, even when he is at his Holy work! The High Priest, too, has his daydreams!"

"No, no, all is lost!" answered the other, all malice now notably absent from his voice and his manner much altered by the burden of the despair he bore. "Hell's legions, I fear, prepare a place for me!"

While they talked Hypup the former Page roused himself from his stupor and stole through the open door into the broad chamber without; availing himself of the guards' keys (which had been left rather carelessly in the cell door) he entered the hallway and set to work emancipating the others. Moving further along this hallway he came to the top of a stairway leading down into a pit in the center of which sat some two dozen men, each chained (some by their wrists, some by their ankles) to a broad iron ring which, attached to nothing, was nevertheless of such substantial weight and such unwieldy and inconvenient configuration that the prisoners seemed to have long since given up all hope of progress and now sat, quite inert.

"Comrades," said Hypup, in little more than a whisper, "fellow prisoners!" and hurried into the pit in a great excitement.

"What's going on?" called one of the prisoners who, shackled by the wrists and wedged between two others, could not turn to observe the action.

"Some boy has just come down," replied another of the prisoners, shackled by his ankles and laying on his belly, and facing the stairway by which Hypup had entered.

"What does he want?" called another.

"I don't know," replied the prisoner on his belly who, despite his professed ignorance, nevertheless spoke with the timbre of *de facto* authority.

"Someone ask him," moaned another.

"I've come to free you," replied Hypup, before any question could be posed or explanation offered.

"He says he's come to free us," said the prisoner laying on his belly, rolling onto his side to face back toward the ring and the others prisoners. "He's got some keys with him."

The boy set to work, and soon succeeded in freeing a half-dozen of those chained. His progress was here interrupted, however, as the last to be freed fell upon one of those still chained, striking and kicking him viciously about the face and body (the as-yet chained prisoner, bound by his wrists, was quite unable to defend himself and lashed out with a series of ineffective kicks which missed his attacker entirely and struck instead those chained around him).

"Stop!" cried Hypup, forgetting the danger of being heard in his surprise and horror. "What on earth are you doing? You must stop this at once!" and here looked to those who had been freed for help, only to discover that they had fled.

"It's no use," said one of the others, bound by his ankles, taking hold of Hypup's own ankle as the former Page stepped near. "Those two were locked in here for quarreling at the King's birthday dinner. I don't imagine that our entreaties will have any impact now."

"But they'll bring the guards!" moaned Hypup, eyeing the exit.

"Have no fear," replied the prisoner. "Free us, as we will overwhelm them with our numbers. Escape is a certainty for some!"

Their conversation was interrupted at this moment by a great cry from the hallway, and a moment later the guards came charging down the staircase. Close on their heels came the three from the prison cells above: the first and second standing tall, shouting bold declarations and threats while the third, streaked in filth, scampered behind them like an animal. The chamber erupted with the noise of the prisoners' shouting and the frantic clinking of their chains against the great ring and stone floor.

"Seize the guards!" cried the prisoners. "Kill them! Bash their heads in! Break their faces! Stomp out their innards! Carve out their eyes! Leave them for the buzzards to feast on!"

"Heaven have mercy!" cried the first guard, doing mortal battle with a prisoner who had jumped on his back and was attempting to choke the life from him.

"God deliver us!" cried the other guard, trying desperately to extricate himself from the pile of prisoners who now fell upon him. "Boy! Save us! Think of the mercy we have shown you! Is this the proper wage of our generous indulgence?"

"What can I do?" cried Hypup, horrified by his act's terrible consequence. And, overwhelmed by a sudden and, it seemed, final aversion to all that he saw (an aversion which, startling in its intensity and clarity, arrived as though the reminder of some truth once understood but since obscured by distraction and circumstance), he abandoned his efforts and fled the prison.

21.
Huetrubutru Returns, Bringing Terrible News

Hassock, the King's Most Trusted Advisor, having recovered from the swoon brought on by the Soothsayer's draught (a swoon which had lasted for three days and three nights, during which the Councilor could find neither sleep nor the waking world, but had rather lingered between them as a soul not yet departed), and finding that it left in its wake a staggering headache, lay convalescing in his chamber, attempting with a series of hot and cold compresses to alleviate his discomfort, when a sudden impertinent knock sounded on the chamber door which, to Hassock's throbbing brain, sounded as a hundred thousand drums being struck at once and he felt, as he had often felt since taking over the position of Most Trusted Advisor from the previous Most Trusted Advisor (a man who had been jailed, the story went, for treason, though it was widely spoken that in fact he had done little more than advise the King that the Kingdom should store crops grown in the summer so that they could be eaten during the winter), that he was being assaulted by something indefinite and horrible whose very existence heralded for him immeasurable hardship and suffering, and whose resolution lay somewhere far beyond the very furthest limit of his own strength and ability.

"What is it!" he cried, more a challenge than a question, and arose in thoughtless readiness to attack whoever entered with the full venom of his present condition.

"My Commander!" cried Huetrubutru, entering with great intention and on rapid steps to kneel at Hassock's feet. "I heartily apologize for whatever annoyance I have caused you by intruding on you here, but I come bearing news of the utmost urgency."

"Yes," replied Hassock, in a voice that was still too loud, and blinking several times, attempting to reconcile the scene before him with the lingering sense that confrontation would soon be required of him. "Yes, I see! Well, very good! Let's have it, then!" and here he slapped the scout on the back in a forced gesture of geniality intended to dispel the lingering pall of aggression and annoyance.

"My Commander," replied Huetrubutru, rising and taking the chair offered him, "the enemy is advancing at an alarming rate. They are already across our borders, and well on their way to that little-known and rarely-used mountain pass which circumvents the Mercurial Swamp and leads past the Infinite Lake. If they have continued at the rate of progress which I observed, I fear that they have already put their heels to the swamp's nearest border and are well on their way to us."

"This is indeed terrible news," replied Hassock, only half listening, for the persistent pain in his head.

"Yes," agreed Huetrubutru, "truly terrible! What shall we do?"

"Naturally the thing to do is dispatch the army," replied Hassock. "But as they have all deserted the Kingdom, and have gone to seek the prize which the King has offered, I fear our only hope is to pray that some disaster befall the enemy such that they are unable to continue."

"As you see fit," replied Huetrubutru, bowing low before the Advisor's superior wisdom. "I laugh at my former trepidation! For, after all: God has put the King upon His throne, and so would not allow any man to overtake it. Some disaster will surely befall them: to fear otherwise is an act of both treason and blasphemy! I beg your pardon, but what is that smell?"

The wind had changed direction, and blew a rotten stench through the perfumed bedchamber.

"I cannot doubt, though I wish I could," replied Hassock, sniffing the befouled air. "It is the irrefutable evidence of the endeavor's folly! Or have you failed to observe the pile of limbs and bodies gathered in the courtyard?"

"I observed it," replied Huetrubutru, covering his nose with his handkerchief, "though I thought it best to stay the rapid course of my thoughts, lest I come to a conclusion contrary to what the King has decreed. Tell me: what says the King?"

"The King says nothing," replied Hassock, falling exhausted upon a couch. "He listens only to the Soothsayer, that poisoning wretch, whose very words I fear may bring misfortune on all of our heads. And, as the Soothsayer says nothing of the bodies, I fear the King is content to let them stay where they are until the crows have picked them clean, and only the bones remain."

"A Kingdom cannot endure in this fashion!" cried Huetrubutru, rising to his feet and unsheathing his sword, as though with it he might strike down the embodied apparition of troubling circumstance.

"Calm yourself," cried Hassock, "and sheathe your sword! Do not think that nothing is being done, that you must hurry with rash and rushed thoughts to strike at the heart of calamity! Even now I am impressing upon the King with subtle touches the path which the Kingdom must follow. Have no fear: all will be made well, and the Kingdom will endure!"

"I am heartily relieved to hear you speak so confidently," replied Huetrubutru. "Forgive my rashness! It is only the lingering memory of that marching force, so vast as to seem nearly infinite, and bearing innumerable weapons before which our castle walls will fall like leaves before the storm, that has inspired my careless and unconsidered behavior. Please: speak not a word of it to the King!"

"You have my word," replied Hassock. "Now go and see your family, I am certain they have missed you, and you them."

After Huetrubutru was gone Hassock fell upon the floor and cursed Heaven, for it did indeed seem incontrovertible that the resolution of the Kingdom's coming hardships lay somewhere beyond the furthest limit of his strength and ability.

22.

Meanwhile, on the Shores of the Infinite Lake

By the time the riot within the dungeon had arisen and been quelled (by the intervention of several stout farmers, who had been in the fields during the King's call for Hazaiah's head and the exodus of the group seeking that prize, and so who had not had the opportunity to make their allegiances, and who had since been deputized, out of dire necessity, into the Royal Guard), and by the time that Huetrubutru had returned bearing his terrible news (by which time also the broad moat, the recent recipient of many severed limbs and crushed bodies, had changed its color by several shades, and lost much of the vegetation that grew along its border to some unknown ailment), the force making its way to Hazaiah's castle had already made several disastrous attempts to cross the Infinite Lake. The first involved rafts made of logs: these tipped easily, and were disturbed by the slightest wave, so that a number of warriors (weighed down by their weapons and armor) and dozens of peasants (who could not swim) were quickly drowned. This disaster produced a violent argument within the remaining group, with one faction asserting that the rafts were sound in principle, and simply required more skillful handling, and the other declaring that the rafts (several dozen had been made, requiring no little effort) should be burned and the whole plan forgotten.

The argument lasted for several days, during which time the bodies of the drowned peasants (who floated freely, unencumbered by any armor or weaponry) continually washed up onto the shore. At night the forest and the canyon echoed with the lamentations of the surviving peasants who, as they had in the forest, had given up all hope of success and resigned themselves to whatever fate befell them. It was a melancholy time, and a few of the warriors fell to lamenting as well, for it seemed that no solution would ever be found. It was then a surprise to everyone when, on the seventh morning, a ship's sails appeared over the far horizon.

"We're saved!" cried the peasants. "God has delivered us! All praises be!" and they fell to dancing and carousing, and drinking what remained of the wine, and fighting amongst themselves over trifles.

When (late in the evening) the ship drew near, the Captain hailed them jovially, and waved from the railing, and rode out himself in the first tender, where he was met by the fat peasant of short stature who had led the assembly through the woods and who, for the time being, remained its leader.

"My friend!" cried the Captain, embracing the peasant and shaking his hand. "What a joy it is to meet a fellow countryman, after a long and arduous journey! If you would but listen, I will tell a tale of such hardship and sorrow that your eyes will exhaust their salty reserves! But come: let's have a glass of your wine, and I will tell you all that I have seen!" and, draping a friendly arm about the bewildered peasant's shoulders, the Captain entered the warriors' camp.

23.
The Captain's Story

"My friends!" said the Captain, after a cup of wine had been called for and received, and also a meal of the best cured meats and dried vegetables that the warriors had in store, and a set of warm and dry clothes, for the Captain had been quite dampened by his journey (for after all, the Captain did not hesitate to remind them, such was the least hospitality one might show to one's countrymen), "My story begins some years ago, when I was but a child on my father's knee! It was a happy and wonderful time: my heart swells to think of it! At every turn I was bathed in my parents' affection, and they showered upon me all the gifts one might bestow upon a visiting dignitary, for such was their vocation! They numbered among the King's Royal Grooms, and were responsible for the pleasure of the King's guests. And honorable in this task they were, for my tongue can hardly illuminate the extent to which these good, honest people served their King! How often was my father called from his bed in the early hours, and sent on some perilous errand? I cannot say: my mind balks at having to remember them all! And how often was my beautiful mother (for indeed she was beautiful, all of the King's guests used to say so!) roused from sleep and called into their chambers in my father's absence? Such loyalty! And how it weighed upon them! For often I stood at that chamber door and listened: how I heard my mother's moans and sighs! What pity it inspired in me! For a woman such as my mother was, resolute and reticent, must be in the throes of profound exhaustion to exclaim so expressively in the company of the King's honored guests. And when she returned, her face reddened and her brow dampened by her labors... How my heart wept, that such loyalty carried so high a tax! But such was their love for the King!

"But I fear that I have tired your ears with this preamble! I will say in summation only that as child to the King's own Grooms I had ample opportunity to observe the manners and graces of those dignitaries who, in their travels, came to stay with us for a time, and I began to conduct myself as a young gentleman should. As such I caught the eye of a young woman, the daughter of a visiting Rajah and heir to a vast fortune in the far East. Oh but that I had been a wiser man, such might have seemed to me like the flower of those carnivorous plants one finds in some parts of the Tropics, whose pleasing appearance (one must learn!) holds danger for any who come too near. Alas, despite my courtly manners I was still unlearned in the ways of Kings and Kingdoms, and in time would suffer greatly for the knowledge. For the young woman's affections I naively returned, and counted myself the lucky star of Heaven's gaze, for seven blessed days and nights, until the King's own guard discovered us upon a velvet couch in a secluded chamber, and my days of happiness came to a sudden and lamentable end!"

Here he drank deeply and with great pathos of the cup before him, and all within earshot hung upon his final word, and considered what terrible fate must have befallen the young lovers, whose uninterrupted happiness each man listening now dearly wished.

"As you may well have guessed," the Captain continued, once his glass had been refilled, "the King and the Rajah were meeting to broker a marriage between the Prince and the Princess (a very advantageous union, for it would join their nations' armies, lands, and fortunes): you might well imagine, then, their outrage when the young Princess spurned the Prince and showered her affections upon me, the Grooms' son! Likewise we were forbidden to see one another, and I received a hundred lashes at the Rajah's own hand, while my parents stood at the King's side, for such was their loyalty! Once my wounds healed I was allowed to return to my duties as Groom Attendant, and as such was made to carry the linens and silks and other fine and rare and precious fabrics from the Royal Tailor to the Rajah's antechamber, beyond which (I knew) stood my beloved Rajah's daughter, her body wrapped in the fabrics that would make her wedding gown (the fabrics that I carried, even as my breaking heart protested!) and her cheeks wet with tears at the thought of the hundred lashes that had troubled my poor backside.

"I ask you, gentle countrymen: has any man here suffered as I have? Has any man suffered a hundred lashes at an outraged father's hand, or been forced to porter the fabrics to make the gown in which his love will marry another?"

All were silent, and several eyes were moved to tears by the Captain's sad story. The fat peasant, who was still in charge, refilled the Captain's glass (which had again been emptied) and said, "Please, continue with your tale!"

"Very well!" cried the Captain. "For seven days and nights I neither slept nor ate; rather my heart and mind raged with anger at the terrible injustice of a world which would force love to subjugate itself to Kingly rule. On the seventh night my racing and disquiet thoughts hatched a madman's scheme, and I imagined in my unwell state that I would rescue my beloved on the very hour of her marriage, that I would enter that cathedral with naked blade (though I knew that such would put my soul at peril!) and cut her from their midst, that we would set sail upon the vast sea and make good our escape... Ah, such is the folly of inexperience!

"The day of the wedding arrived, and I shirked my duties and hid behind the cathedral's great altar. There I waited until the very hour of the wedding. At last all were assembled, and the Priest raised his arms to call those present to prayer: at that moment I leapt forth, my sword unsheathed, thinking only of my beloved. But alas! So well did I hide behind the altar that none had detected my presence throughout the morning's preparations; likewise I had witnessed none of the alterations those preparations had made upon that Holy room until the moment I boldly revealed myself. The platform had been covered with flowers of all kinds, and as I stepped out among them I lost my footing and fell in a foolish heap. I attempted to rise, but found no clear footing: also my legs had fallen asleep due to the uncomfortable crouch in which I had spent the morning, and would not behave as I wished them to.

"While I attempted to regain my footing the crowd erupted in a frenzy of outrage. The Royal Guards, the

Rajah's own guards, and the Prince himself had all drawn their swords and were advancing on me steadily, while the King and Rajah stood at some distance behind them, calling for my head. I caught a fleeting glimpse of my beloved, but at the sight of bared steel her attendants had taken her by the hand, and she was pulled from the room. She made one attempt to free herself and join me, but she was quickly taken up again and carried from my sight.

"Had I known then that this would be my final vision of her, I might well have fallen upon my sword! Alas, youth is full of the fire of love, and imagines that its passion holds some power that the world can never overcome. I fancied that I would carve a path to her, that we would escape together and be happy. But at the moment I arose brandishing my sword the Priest threw himself between the guards and I, protesting that there should be no blood shed in God's Holy Sanctuary. The poor man's timing was tragically impeccable! My sword, rising in an arc, neatly opened the poor Priest's belly; his guts fell out upon the floor and his screams filled the high and Holy chamber.

"This unhappy accident redoubled the outrage of all present. I knew then that my beloved was lost to me forever, that my bold plan had failed, and that I had relinquished not only my life but also my very soul in my vain and bloody attempt. A black despair overcame me, and I threw myself through the handsome and ornate window that formed the room's head, hoping to end my miserable life. I fell a great distance, and was swallowed by the moat; my lungs' protest fought valiantly, and finally overcame my heart's wish (that I be drowned, and spared the pain of consequence); I swam ashore in a hail of arrows and, mounting a horse which stood nearby, I put the Kingdom to my heels and have never returned, until now."

All wept at the Captain's sad story, and the Captain's glass was filled, and another plate of food brought. The fat peasant, who was still in charge, blew his nose on his sleeve and dried his eyes and asked, "But what happened to the Rajah's daughter? Did you never return to rescue her from the Prince?"

"She was married to the Prince," replied the Captain, "just as soon as a new Priest could be found. They were married a year. After a year she had failed to provide the Prince with a son, and so he sent her to the Royal Doctor. The Royal Doctor prescribed to her a series of treatments, many involving the burned or powderized male organs of various animals, and she became sick and died in terrible agony. I received word (my mother and father, who refused to disown me despite my blasphemy and treason, and who as a result of my act were cast out of Castle life and forced to live as peasants, nevertheless wrote to me often, sending their letters to ports through which I was likely to pass) the very morning upon which I intended to sail for home, a hired army at my back and love in my heart. You cannot imagine my sorrow! For not only had my beloved died in writhing agony, but also I had no money to pay the brigands I had hired (I had expected rather to raid the Royal coffers, once the Prince was dead at my hand). Likewise they tore my ship apart, taking everything of value, leaving me penniless and doubly heartbroken. Oh, merciless fate!"

"Poor man!" cried the fat peasant, who was still in charge, as he refilled the Captain's glass.

"Yes," cried the Captain, in a much louder voice, "my pain is deep and unquenchable! Woe be to any man who stands before me!"

24.
While the Captain Told His Story...

While the Captain told his story the sun set, and in the darkness the crew of the ship tendered silently ashore and encircled the camp. At the Captain's signal ("Woe be to any man who stands before me!") they fell upon the assembly, killing and wounding warrior and peasant alike. A great screaming and crying rent the still night, and carried along the empty water, and echoed between the high, sheer canyon walls.

"We are tricked!" cried Hafafanot, unsheathing his sword and plunging it into the Captain's belly with great ease, for the Captain was preoccupied with the task of killing the fat peasant, who after all was still in charge.

"I am killed!" cried the fat peasant, bleeding from a great wound to his chest. "Friends, brothers, save my wretched life!"

"Good companions!" cried the Captain, "bear me back aboard the ship, for I fear that I am killed as well!"

At this request a group of four rushed in on Hafafanot, forcing him to retreat, and hoisted the Captain between them. But with the Captain on their shoulders they could neither turn about nor effectively wield their weapons, and they were soon cut down where they stood. The Captain fell atop them, Hafafanot's sword still protruding from his middle.

"Oh merciless fate!" cried the Captain, and then lay still.

"Leave no man alive!" cried Hafafanot, retrieving his sword.

The battle raged for several hours, and several dozen were killed and wounded, and the shoreline became sodden with the blood of the fallen and littered with the severed limbs of the wounded. Finally the sun crested the horizon, and the combatants saw each other clearly, and saw too that the sailors had all been killed, and so they lowered their weapons and fell to speculating amongst themselves how long it had been since the last sailor was killed, and how long they had been fighting no enemy but one another (for such mistakes can happen in a group so large, and in the dark) and all present, even those wounded and barely clinging to life, had to laugh. Then they broke camp and boarded the ship, though the sky grew dark and menacing, and set sail for the far shore, with the tenders tethered behind loaded with the peasants who did not fit onboard. Far out on the open water the storm broke, and the waves grew tall and came over the rail, and several warriors were swept overboard and sank to the depths, and all of the tenders were overturned and all of the peasants aboard them were drowned. The mast was broken in two, and the great sail torn, and all hands abandoned their stations and fell to repenting their sins and begging for mercy from their Heavenly Father. A hurricane wind arose, and several of those repenting and begging for mercy were blown overboard, and others were blown into the rigging, where their bones were broken and where some became entangled and had the life choked from them. Finally after several hours the storm relented, and the ship drifted quite impotently upon the open water, for two days and two nights, until by chance it ran aground on the far shore, and all aboard disembarked and fell upon the sandy ground, praising God and His infinite mercy.

25.
While They Sailed...

While they sailed the opposing force (which, despite all calamity, still consisted of several hundred soldiers, one-quarter of which rode on horseback, leading a column of catapults, cannons, and fortified towers, which were followed by a column of several hundred more soldiers, of which nearly half rode on horseback, which was itself followed by a number of experimental implements designed to tear down high walls), having traveled via a rarely-used mountain passage so as to avoid the Mercurial Swamp, passed not one hundred miles north of the Infinite Lake.

"Bit of rough weather to the south," said the Commander, considering the clouds, and nervously tapping the side of his helmet with the flat of his saber. "I shouldn't like to be out in it, if it comes this way!"

"Have no fear, Great Leader," said the robed figure beside him, who had only recently joined the procession. "On my journey I observed a cat that had been crushed beneath the wheels of an oxcart. It's belly had burst in such a way as to form the shape of a lion's face, and the blood it spilled made a regal mane. This is a powerful omen, and promises victory to the King whose standard bears the lion!"

"Well, yes, that is nice to hear," said the Commander, still considering the clouds, and removing his helmet to mop at his perspiring and rather bald scalp.

"Better to have the omens with you than against you, I suppose. No harm in a little sorcering, so long as no one gets hurt. And after all: you've got to earn a living, haven't you? Yes, you do, yes you do." All of this he spoke distractedly, turning first one way and then the other, then quickly back again, as though constantly changing his mind, convinced that it was not the situation he beheld but the one occurring out of the corner of his eye which required his full attention. "In any event," he said finally, returning his helmet to his head and facing decidedly forward, "there's little to be done about it, one way or the other. We've already come this far, and the King demands it, and the men expect it, so there's really nothing more to say."

"Of course," replied the Soothsayer. "Your tactical genius is certainly unrivaled, to speak so eloquently and with such decision. The men are lucky to have one such as yourself in command."

"I've always thought so," replied the Commander, still facing forward, but smiling nonetheless. "Did you know: I was first in my class at the Military Academy. We had to devise a method for laying siege to a castle vast enough to grow food and shelter livestock, and with a spring of clean fresh water at its heart, and a high and fortified wall surrounding it: an unassailable fortress! Out of the entire class, only my strategy was picked by a panel of Professors and Military Advisors. It was quite an honor, and I was immediately promoted to my present rank." He had grown rather red in the face while he spoke, and now stopped to calm himself and catch his breath.

"What was your plan, if I may be so bold as to inquire?" asked the Soothsayer. "I imagine that I might learn much, kneeling at the foot of your intellect."

"It was no great matter," replied the Commander, his chest swelling with pride. "Since it was impossible to starve their army, I therefore strategized to starve my own army - or, more accurately, a quarter of my own army, the quarter tenting along the front lines and most visible to the enemy. Then it was simply a matter of waiting for the castle's inhabitants to tire of our presence, and convince themselves that a force so weakened could be easily overcome or inspired to retreat, and open their gates to make some attack of their own. Then we would fall upon them, we who were not starving, and enter through the gate, and take the castle in one bold and masterful maneuver!"

"A brilliant plan," said the Soothsayer, applauding.

At that moment an eagle flew down from the heavens and plucked a soldier's cap from his head. All watched, amazed. The Commander asked the Soothsayer what import this miraculous occurrence held. The Soothsayer had not been watching, however, and could make no reply. Further along the trail the cap was discovered in the low branches of a nearby tree, and was retrieved with little effort. The Soothsayer explained to the soldier that such a sign meant that he would return home with his faculties intact. Later that night the soldiers fell to quarreling amongst themselves, and the soldier whose cap had been returned was struck with a burning log and blinded in one eye. It seemed better, however, and they all agreed, not to bring this to the attention of the Soothsayer, who they feared this contradiction might anger, and whose power they nevertheless held in reverence, and who in either case had not been seen for some time. In the morning the storm that had troubled the lake hung over them, and the sun could not be seen, and the wind blew the blinded soldier's cap from his head, and it was lost and could not be found.

"I wish the Soothsayer was here," muttered the Commander, nervously striking his helmet with the flat of his saber. "Then we'd know what all this is about. Does God want us to win, or doesn't He? It's too much for a man to ponder."

After three days the rain stopped, though the clouds remained overhead, and the army continued on, moving sluggishly in muddy footing, with everyone sniffling and sneezing and feeling feverish and achy.

"This will never do," said the Commander. "No, this will never do at all. At this rate, everyone will be too sick to fight."

This prospect greatly troubled the Commander, and he did not sleep for two nights. By noon on the third day they crested the final mountain ridge, and saw below them the Great Forest, and the Commander was greatly relieved that soon his men would travel beneath the shelter of hanging boughs, and no longer need to hunt for shelter on the high, exposed buttes and passes.

They had great difficulty in descending, and several pack animals lost their footing and tumbled to their deaths, carrying their loads down into low and inaccessible valleys where they could not be retrieved. This the men greatly lamented, for several of the animals were favorites of this or that solider, and regardless carried many comforts whose absence was sorely felt. But these misfortunes were forgotten when, at nightfall, the army entered the forest. Fires were made and meals prepared, and the men fell to joking and gambling, and the Commander removed his helmet and fell into a deep and tranquil sleep, certain (in his relief and fatigue, and even in the absence of the Soothsayer's say-so) that their good fortune was God's doing, and that He had undoubtedly bestowed His favor upon their campaign.

26.

Page and Master

Meanwhile, not forty miles away, Hypup the former Page and escaped prisoner sat beside the fire he had managed to build, eating the small meal he had managed to prepare and listening with concern to the distant sounds from the army encampment (which, despite the distance, carried to him as faint but unmistakable din), when out of the shadows beyond the firelight there appeared a figure, approaching rapidly, its face contorted into so hideous an expression (and with a nose so smashed and misshapen) that Hypup mistook it at once for some wild animal, intent on his destruction. He let out a cry and, toppling off the log on which he sat, struck his head on an exposed root with such force that he forgot his fear in his pain, and did not remember it for several moments, after which it seemed strange that a wild animal would not have finished its assault, and he sat up and considered the haggard and somewhat bloodied man now crouching over his fire, eating his supper.

"Hello," said Hypup, rubbing the lump now growing on his head. "I beg your pardon for crying out as I did, but you did give me a terrific scare, which I'm sure might have been avoided if you had simply made some salutation to announce your presence. You would have been more than welcome to join me by the fire, if I'd only had the chance to see you and invite you."

"Delightful," said the peasant, between mouthfuls. "Splendid. Awfully nice of you."

"Excuse me," said Hypup, after another moment had passed, "but I don't suppose you would mind leaving some of that for me. I went through an awful lot of work catching it, and building the fire with which to cook it, and I am awfully hungry, as I've been in prison for some time, and was given very little to eat."

"Perfectly reasonable," replied the peasant, chewing with gusto.

"Excuse me," said Hypup, a bit more forcefully, after yet another moment had passed, in which the peasant had not slackened the pace of his consumption, and in which Hypup was forced to contemplate the woefully diminished and diminishing contents of the spit the peasant held clutched in his hands. "I'll ask you to give my dinner back to me, if you don't mind. I have no great wish to quarrel with you, but you leave me with little recourse." And here he lifted a great branch from the fire, and menaced the peasant with the burning end.

"All right," said the peasant, halting his consumption for the first time since his arrival, but otherwise giving the former Page and his burning implement as little regard as possible. "If you feel so strongly about it, you should have simply said so in the first place. I've no intention of overreaching the courtesy which any traveler, in this country at least, might expect, but if you say that's what I've done then I will leave and trouble you no more." Here he held the spit out to the former Page who, in receiving it, found it necessary to put down the burning branch which, due to his and its size, he had been forced to wield with both hands.

"Thank you ever so much," said the former Page, with a note of disappointment, for it was clear from the spit's diminished heft (and closer inspection by the firelight only confirmed his fears) that much of the carcass had been relieved of its meager store. What meat he did find he fell upon with great appetite, and did not notice as the peasant took his leave, and so was troubled by pangs of regret at his own inhospitality when he looked up and found himself alone. "Wait!" he cried, uncertain of which direction the peasant took and so uncertain where to stand and where to call. "Wait, please! You must forgive my rudeness, but I was rather hungry from my prolonged ordeal! If you would only return, I would show you the kindest hospitality I can command in such humble circumstances, and see to it that you want for nothing which I am in a position to provide!"

"You speak like one of good stature and noble bearing," said the peasant, emerging from the forest off to the former Page's right. "I accept your invitation." And, reentering the ring of firelight, he plucked the spit from the former Page's hands and made short work of the meat that remained. "Now please tell me," he said, discarding the emptied spit into the shadows, "how did one such as yourself, and by that I mean one who now finds himself alone in the woods, with no home to return to and no friend on whom to call, come to possess the manners of a courtier?"

"I would gladly tell," replied the former Page, "if those same courtly manners did not expressly advise against the bemoaning of hardships while amongst pleasant company. Still, since we are well outside the walls and realms of the court, and since I am I imagine miserable enough to not care a hang about the court and its ways, and since I have in any case been forever banned from the court (the court which, from my youngest days, was my dearest love and the seat of all of my highest aspirations!) I will perhaps allow myself some little leeway, only because it has been requested, and it is always rude to deny a request."

"Yes," said the peasant, uncertain what sort of response was expected of him after such a prolonged preamble. "Yes, very well. Fine then. Go on. I'm all ears."

"Oh, sore hardship and travail!" cried the former Page, beating his breast with such unexpected violence that the peasant started back in alarm. "Would that I were a poet, I might unpack my heart with such lyrical mastery as to justly give tongue to my sorrow and pain!" and here he nevertheless relayed with great passion and feeling the innumerable injustices and miseries he had suffered, including but not limited to his unexpected imprisonment and subsequent escape, and the discovery that his parents were missing and, if the blood on the floor was any indication, very likely murdered, but perhaps most of all that now his heart's truest wish (to mingle with the fine people of the King's court, and learn their fine manners, and bask in their finery) could never again be realized. He then fell to bitter weeping, and soon forgot himself in his sadness, and began to moan and wail, and make such a terrific noise that the peasant soon feared that some member of the nearby army, straying far afield in search of food, might overhear them and report their presence to his Commander.

"Calm yourself!" the peasant cried, "and dry your eyes, for I will tell you a tale which will soon lighten your dreary mood! I tell you now that God has smiled on you in your plight, for I am myself descended from that very noble court of which you so adoringly speak. Yes, I know that my appearance speaks my story false! Yet I swear on the bones of my noble ancestors that a nobleman's blood runs in my veins! Indeed, amongst all of the nobles at court you will find none more noble than I!"

"I do not wish to quarrel with you any more than is necessary," replied the former Page, who had ceased his wailing to listen to the peasant's story, "but I must say I find it extremely unlikely that one of such disheveled and unpleasant - if you don't mind me saying so - appearance and manner is descended from nobles, and more at home in the court than behind a plough; still, I hate to call any man a liar, for such is considered extremely rude, even amongst the lower classes, and so will withhold my judgement until your story is finished."

"I humbly thank you," replied the peasant, rising to his feet and bowing low in a gross exaggeration of courtly courtesy, "and lament that life has brought me to such poor circumstances that I am suspected of deceit when I attempt to say that I am myself; still, such suspicion is fully justified, and I cannot begrudge you your good prudence, and so I thank you instead that you offer me your ear: a man in my position can hope for little more!"

"Yes," replied the former Page. "Well. Fine then. Please go on."

"I was born within the Castle walls," the peasant began. "Oh happy days of youth! My mother was the most beautiful woman in all the land; my father was the bravest warrior! We lived a life of ease and luxury, until the King died and his wretched son took the throne."

"Oh, that days of happiness could endure forever!" cried the former Page. "What happened to you then?"

"My mother, as I said, was the most beautiful woman in the land," continued the peasant, "and as such the new King wanted her for his Queen. Likewise he sent my father on a fool's errand, an errand that carried him across seven oceans and eventually precipitated his demise at the hands of a tribe of vicious cannibals. My mother, inconsolable, vowed never to wed another, a vow which inspired the new King to court her relentlessly and then, when these efforts proved futile, to strip her of my father's rank and lands and cast us, nearly destitute, from the gilded gates and upon the barren and merciless world!" Here the peasant broke down, and wept with such passion for such a prolonged interval that the former Page forsook his previous suspicion and knelt before the fallen nobleman.

"But tell me your name, good Nobleman," entreated the former Page, "and I will pledge myself to you and be your Page until your days have ended, and you have rendered forth your soul to God, who lent it."

"My name," replied the peasant, ending his lamentations with swiftness and ease, and drawing himself up to his full height, "is Herarityrarity, son of Herarityrarityrarity, grandson of Herarity the Honorable, great-grandson of Herarity the Kind, and a dozen other landed nobles stretching back to the time before the Kingdom was unified and the tribes still quarreled amongst themselves. And as to your request, as I find myself in a position wherein I must consider a convicted criminal for my Page, I am moved to accept your offer only because you have shared with me your meal, and I take you to be an honest child, in spite of your criminal past, and so welcome you with fewer reservations than I might."

"What luck!" cried the Page, jumping at once to his feet and embracing his new Master. "God has indeed smiled on me in my sorrowful plight! To think that only an hour ago I had nothing: no family, no home, only my meager dinner and my freedom!"

"Yes, yes," replied Herarityrarity, eyeing the collection of leaves and soft grasses the Page had collected and distributed beneath the cover of a particularly thick convergence of low-hanging boughs. "Now, as it is getting rather late, and I fear I hear the rumblings of distant thunder, I will leave you to the prayers of thanksgiving which I am certain you are shortly to offer, and bid you goodnight, as my various hardships have afflicted me with a terrible lethargy."

"Of course!" said the Page, moving out of the peasant's way and offering, with a grand flourish, the bed he had made. "Allow me only one final display of gratitude." And here he knelt and kissed the peasant's ragged shoes, embracing and caressing them as one might one's dearest sweetheart. "And now goodnight, and sleep soundly and with pleasant dreams!"

The peasant made no reply, but nestled into the rustic bed and was soon snoring. The Page situated himself outside, and listened to the sound with adoration. After a while the wind began to blow, and a few raindrops to fall, and the Page moved closer to the fire and prayed that the storm would pass. No sooner had he uttered this prayer, however, than lighting split the sky, and the rain began to fall in earnest, and the fire was quickly doused. The Page, wet and shivering, crawled beneath the boughs, where he received a kick and a sharp rebuke from his Master. Venturing without he hid himself as best he could from the relentless and indifferent rain, and in this fashion passed the night, until the sun rose and chased the storm from the heavens. In the early gray light he set about searching for food, and discovered some berries in a patch nearby, and a pair of plump bird's eggs in a nest, and returned with these to find his Master awake and hungry after his night of rest.

He had great difficulty, however, in restarting the fire, and his Master became grievously annoyed with him, and ate all of the berries, and threatened to find another Page. After what felt like a very long time the kindling began to burn, and the Page breathed a sigh of relief, and cooked the eggs in their shells, and handed them to his Master with great pride and gratitude swelling his heart, for only a day before he had had nothing at all, and now he had a Master, and he still could not believe his luck.

27.

In the Courtyard, Two Guards Were Talking

In the Castle's courtyard, two guards were talking.

"Great gravy," said one to the other. "Something has to be done about these bodies: they stink to high Heaven!"

"I couldn't agree with you more," replied the second. "If it gets any worse I think I'm going to be sick. I don't know how the King can stand it!"

"Beats me," agreed the first. "And on top of that, they look something awful! What if a foreign dignitary comes to visit? What would they think? It's no way for civilized people to live!"

"You're right there," said the second, poking at the nearest corpse with the butt of his spear. At this pressure the rather bloated body burst, releasing a foul collection of entrails and an attendant stink powerful enough to send both of the guards fleeing from the place, retching and gagging.

"Why on earth would you do that?" asked the first of the second, when he had recovered his composure somewhat. "Great God in Heaven!"

"I'm sorry," said the second, still looking rather green, "I had no idea that was going to happen."

"Well that about does it," said the first, considering the pile. "They couldn't move the bodies now, even if they wanted to! And in any event, it's a problem for the Royal Engineers: there's nothing for us to do about it."

"Truly spoken," replied the second.

At that moment one of the Royal Engineers happened to walk through the gate and pass through the courtyard near to where the guards were standing. The first guard hailed him, and asked him what he thought could be done about the corpses. The Engineer replied that the only problems of concern to him were the ones outlined by the King Himself; therefore, as the problem of what to do with the corpses had not been brought to his attention by the King, or indeed by anybody in any position of rank, as far as he was concerned the problem did not exist.

"You see," he went on, rather unnecessarily, as the guards had completely lost interest, as it had become clear that nothing would come of the conversation, "a problem that is not problematic is *ipso facto* no problem at all. The King has the eyes of an eagle, and the nose of a prized hunting hound: if He finds nothing offensive in this situation then it is not for us, the lesser subjects, to question and quarrel: rather we must meditate upon that Kingly wisdom that finds nothing objectionable in so grotesque a sight, and ponder how we might become more like Him!"

"That's all well and good," replied the first guard, "but I have to say that perhaps the only reason the King hasn't taken offense is that He's way up in His high tower. If He were down here next to the pile, He might change his Royal tune."

"He means no offense," the second guard added quickly. "It's just that we have to spend all day here, and the pile smells worse by the hour."

"If you feel that something simply must be done," said the Engineer with apparent annoyance, "then I suggest you draft a formal notice and deliver it to the Office of Maintenance and Catastrophe Avoidance. You'll have to have it stamped and sealed by the Royal Notary, of course, and signed by two members of the Committee on Castle Affairs, but I'm sure you know how all of that works! In fact, you know so much better than the King, I wonder why you stopped me at all!" and here, with a great flourish of his cape, he turned on his heel and continued on his way.

"An odd sort of fellow," said the first guard to the second, when the Engineer was gone.

"Yes," agreed the second, "and not as helpful as one might hope. Still: now we know what must be done."

"Yes," agreed the first, "for all the good it does us. I, for one, have no idea where the Office of Maintenance and Catastrophe Avoidance is, although I assume that it lies within the inner courtyard, and perhaps within the body of the Castle itself, into which neither of us is allowed. On top of that, I've never even seen a member of the Committee on Castle Affairs, and doubt very much that you have, either."

"You're right, of course," replied the second, turning once again to face the pile, with an attitude of absolute defeat and despair, as though the pile was an adversary which no effort could overcome. Then, after several minutes, and with a great sigh, he said: "I suppose that the stink is not really all that bad, once you've grown accustomed to it, and the sight is unlikely to get any worse. Suppose we keep watch over here, where the befouled wind is unlikely to reach us, and leave the bigger problems to those elected to deal with them."

"There is wisdom in that, certainly," agreed the first. "Further, I would be very surprised if those in charge did not attempt some resolution on their own, before too much time has passed. The King may have the eyes of an eagle and the nose of a hunting dog, but I imagine most everyone else has eyes and noses like our own."

"Well said," replied the second.

Feeling much better about the situation in general, they sheltered into the corner where the wind hardly reached them. Soon, they agreed, they had grown so accustomed to the smell that it was as if there was no smell at all. They felt certain that very soon the problem would be resolved, that it was in more capable hands than their own, and that there was nothing they should do but wait. That afternoon the sky grew dark, and the westward-traveling storm blew hard against them, and the courtyard was flooded with several inches of rainwater with which the pile's foul discharge mingled and by which it was dispersed across the flagstones and out into the moat beyond the wall. The murky sludge remained for two days, and the guards stood their posts with submerged feet, and on the third day noticed red and black sores forming on their ankles, which bled when prodded. The village Doctor was summoned, and a course of treatments advised, the principal component of which involved red-hot coals being applied to the lesions. On the fifth day the lesions had grown and spread, and the guards coughed and vomited uncontrollably, and complained alternately of heat and cold. On the sixth morning, however, those afflicted assured those caring for them that they felt much better, and indeed felt no pain at all. This was of great concern to these attendants, for the lesions had nearly doubled in size overnight, and now gave off a powerful, rotten smell. The village Doctor was again summoned, and the lesions prodded, and the skin across them broke, and the guards were transported suddenly in great pain, and fidgeted on their beds, and in so doing broke open the other sores, and they bled to death from their many wounds, writhing in great agony.

The Priest was summoned, and the bodies examined, and it was decided that the mysterious affliction was the work of the Devil, and that accordingly the guards could not be buried on Holy Ground. This caused much weeping and consternation amongst the families of the deceased, and much protestation, for the guards had always been noble and true, and attended church every Sunday, and always had a coin for the collection, even when there was no food on the table. At this the Priest only shook his head, and explained that it was out of his hands. This failed to satisfy the families, who took the matter before the village Judge. The village Judge, however, explained that since the guards had worked within the Castle, and their illness and subsequent demise had occurred as a direct consequence of their employment, the matter was entirely out of his jurisdiction, and that the wives and families would have to make their complaint at the Office of Castle-Village relations, which was situated in the Castle Affairs building, which was within the Castle's inner courtyard, for which they would need a special pass, available only from one of the members of the Committee on Castle Affairs, none of which he knew. At this the families fell to weeping, and several to scratching at the sores forming on their own hands and arms, which they had only just noticed. The Doctor was sent for but begged off, as he had discovered sores of his own, and was busily attempting various treatments.

Meanwhile, in the tower high above, the King sniffed the air: he was certain he had smelled something only a moment before, but now found that the wind had carried it off. He wondered, briefly, what it could have been. He reassured himself that likely it was nothing of concern and, thus satisfied, sat down to eat his lunch.

28.
On the Eastern Shore of the Infinite Lake

The survivors of the disastrous crossing remained in their camp on the eastern shore of the Infinite Lake for three days, eating what food they had and recovering from their ordeal. On the fourth day the bloated bodies of the drowned began to wash ashore, and the encampment was suffused with their stench, and several of the warriors proclaimed that it was time to leave. This proclamation was met by outraged protest from the peasants, who felt it indecent to leave the bloated dead where they lay. The ensuing argument carried on for several hours, and seemed near to violence, but was finally resolved peacefully by the suggestion that those wishing to stay and bury the dead should do so, and those wishing to continue on should do so, as in this fashion neither faction needed to surrender its position to the other. A tally was taken, and three-quarters of the surviving peasants elected to stay behind, and one quarter of the surviving warriors, saying that with the force so reduced success seemed unlikely, and that they would just as soon go home. Those continuing on took their leave, and traveled for a night and a day to the valley's mouth, and there entered the Mercurial Swamp, wherein a number of peasants were claimed by sinkholes and poisonous snakes, and a few of the warriors were set upon by great cats, which pounced on them from above and killed them with great ferocity. At night the swamp was alive with animal cries and hoots and howls, and the group clung close together, and even the warriors wept with fear. Soon they became lost, and in the dim light confused night and day, and dawn and evening, and became convinced that they would never see the sun or stand on solid ground again. But after several days of aimless wandering the ground grew firm beneath their feet, and they entered into a forest, and then emerged onto a field, and begged of the first farmer they saw the name of the vassal ruling the lands on which they stood.

"These land belong to Hazaiah," replied the farmer, "and it is to him that we pay our tithes, and it is he who presides over the weddings of our sons and daughters, and he who kills the spring's first lamb, and he who makes God's face shine upon us with his prayers."

Hearing the name, the weary and bedraggled assembly fell to weeping, and giving thanks unto God, and praising Him and His mercy. The warriors embraced the peasants, and the peasants embraced each other, and they danced and sang songs, while the farmer continued to seed the ground around them. Finally, when the first blush of their mirth had cooled, they strode forward with renewed energy and restored spirits, and entered into a town, and boarded at the first inn they came to, and ordered food and drink, and it was some time before anyone thought to mention the errand on which they had come, and the nearly innumerable logistical obstacles it presented.

29.
Hazaiah

As the warriors fell to discussing the difficult task
before them, and proposing plans, and arguing amongst
themselves, Hazaiah, vassal of the Kingdom's
easternmost province, officiator of weddings and killer
of lambs, lay reclining upon a divan, alternately dozing
and waking, and when awake alternately singing little
songs to himself and eating from the great plate set
beside him (on a low table designed specifically for the
purpose of holding a plate within easy reach of one
reclining), and when asleep alternately dreaming of one
chambermaid or another, and when in between
wakefulness and sleep alternately sighing deeply and
coughing violently, for he often dozed with food still in
his mouth, and inhaled it most troublingly, so that the
Doctor in his private employ worried over it endlessly,
and lost sleep over it, and had begun to develop an ulcer
as a result of his constant concern, though he was still
very young, and there was no history of ulcers in his
family, and had issued specific instructions to every
carpenter in the region that none should not make any
table of such low stature as to conveniently hold a plate
for one reclining on a divan, though these instructions
were routinely ignored, for the Doctor held less
influence than the vassal Lord, and regardless it was an
easy enough thing for any craftsman to shorten any
table, no matter how exactly the carpenter followed the

Doctor's instructions, and new tables routinely appeared, no matter how vigilantly the Doctor had them destroyed.

"Rum, tum, teetum," sang Hazaiah, waking and plucking from the great plate a succulent morsel, "tum, teetum, teetum, teetum."

"Sire!" said the Head of the Guard, entering abruptly and with no announcement, and startling the rotund and recumbent regent, who fell at once to coughing and sputtering, and attempting with various and discordant acts to dislodge the gobbet now wedged in his windpipe.

"May the Devil take all carpenters, and the Good Lord hide every handsaw!" cried the Doctor, entering on the Head of the Guard's heels, and striking the back of the now kneeling patient with such force that the tidbit was expelled onto the ornate rug. "If I've told Milord once I've told him a thousand times, one must never eat when one is on one's back! The human throat is not designed for chewing and swallowing in that posture! I fear that one day I will not be handy with a whack!" and here he struck the regent's rather thick shoulder a second time for good measure.

"Don't lecture me," replied Hazaiah, rising with difficulty, and with the aid of both Guard and Doctor. "I am not some schoolboy in need of a lesson. Besides," he went on, turning to face the Head of the Guard, "it's this idiot's fault. How many times have I told you never to rush in like that? You're just as likely to frighten a man to death."

"I apologize, Milord," replied the Head of the Guard, coloring deeply under the Doctor's harsh stare. "I have news of a rather urgent nature, and thought it best to inform You with all possible haste."

"There is nothing, I assure you," said the Doctor, stepping between his patient and the Guard, and speaking in a level tone belying his deep underlying outrage, "so pressing and urgent as our Dear Lord's health and wellbeing. If, in the future, you find that you are charged with another, similar piece of news, I urge you to weigh it's value against the primary concern, which I have just mentioned, and see if you still find it deserving of such rash and reckless delivery."

"You are right, of course," replied the Head of the Guard, assuming his proper military posture and facing the Doctor with such unwavering attention that the Doctor's composure faltered and he was inclined to look away. "I have entered only to inform Milord that a small band of strangers, some of whom appear to be warriors, has entered the lands from the Mercurial Swamp, and is presently boarding at an inn near the place, and no one knows what they want or what they are doing here, and some of the villagers think that they may be from Isthinrod."

"And for this you interrupt our Lord at His leisure, and almost cause Him dire harm?" replied the Doctor, rediscovering his outrage somewhere in the Guard's explanation. "The gossip of villagers is a matter for the villagers! Do not think - ,"

"Oh shut up," said Hazaiah, seating himself once again upon the divan and drawing from the great pile a large golden tart. "If there are strangers in my lands, let them be welcomed as any one of us would wish to be welcomed as a stranger upon an unfamiliar shore. Guard, go to the inn where they are boarding with all possible haste, and inform them that they are to be guests in my home for so long as they remain in my lands. Then inform the servants: tonight we feast in welcome and celebration!"

"Milord, I regret that I must question the wisdom of such an invitation!" said the Doctor, once the Head of the Guard had gone. "After all: what if the men in question are indeed from Isthinrod? What if they are scouts of the enemy? What if they wish Your Lordship some grievous harm?"

"Oh, pish posh," replied Hazaiah, gobbling the last of the tart. "Would an enemy enter into my lands like a bumbling vagrant, and shelter at an inn in full view of everyone? Use your head, good Doctor! And further, Isthinrod lies to the *east*, and the Mercurial Swamp lies to the *west*: it is therefore a geographic impossibility that these men have come from Isthinrod!"

"As usual, I must defer to Your superior wisdom in matters both civic and military," replied the Doctor, though distractedly, for he was busily engaged in the not insignificant task of removing from the low table the piled plates, and transferring them to another table, which was higher than the other and farther from the divan. "Certainly You know better than I who is to be trusted and who is to be suspected." Then, lifting the low and now emptied table, he made his exit, grunting and sweating under his burden.

When he was gone Hazaiah rang for the craftsman, who arrived some short time later with his assistant. Together the two moved the taller table to the place that Hazaiah specified, beside the divan. Then, one steadying the top and the other working the saw, they shortened the legs so that the table's contents could be easily reached by one reclining. Hazaiah, much delighted by their workmanship, awarded them each a gold coin and a pastry from his store. Then, bidding them good day, he lay back in his accustomed pose and was soon snoring, a half-chewed strudel dribbling from his lips.

30.
The Cabinet of Advisors

While the courier traveled with all possible haste to deliver Hazaiah's invitation (and while, accordingly, the advancing army moved further into the Great Forest, and the Page attended to his Master, and the band on the eastern shore of the Infinite Lake buried the dead) the various noblemen comprising the Cabinet of Advisors made their way (some very slowly, for some were very old, and had served the King's father before him) into the appointed chamber overlooking the central courtyard to begin their bimonthly meeting.

"I call this meeting to order," said the Secretary. "Orders on hand for the day are as follows: the Cook has stopped making that peach cobbler that everyone enjoys so much, and says that he will not make any more until his brother's cow, which was claimed in a tax last season, is returned."

"Return the cow," said one of the others. "All in favor?" A chorus of support filled the chamber at this prompt. "There you have it," continued the Advisor. "Next order of business, if you please."

"That is all well and good," replied the Secretary, raising his voice somewhat to be heard over the din of congratulations being offered around, "but naturally the cow was put to the slaughter and enjoyed, I have no doubt, by many of us here. So there's really nothing to be done about it."

"Suppose," said one of the Elder Advisors, "that we simply give the Cook's brother another cow? Would that satisfy him?" A chorus of affirmative votes filled the room, and the resolution was passed in short order. "There, you see?" said the Elder Advisor to the Secretary. "We didn't have all of this hemming and hawing in my days as Secretary. If a thing had to be done, we simply saw that it was done!"

"Very nice," replied the Secretary. "I do appreciate everyone's enthusiasm on the point. Unfortunately, this has already been attempted. The Cook's brother was very partial to this particular cow, it seems, and no other cow will do."

"Well," said the Elder Advisor. But then, having nothing else to offer, he fell silent.

"What if," said the very youngest Advisor, with a nervous tone that bespoke his inexperience, "what if we simply painted another cow to look like he cow that was lost? Would the Cook's brother know the difference?"

"An excellent suggestion," rejoined the Advisor sitting beside the Cabinet's youngest member.

"Yes," said the Secretary, "it might be, but this has already been attempted as well. It seems that the cow in question gave milk of a particular sweetness, which no other cow has been able to reproduce. We've had the Royal Alchemist at work on the problem, and so far he has been unable to create any similar effect, although he did cause one cow to give milk in a fantastic array of brilliant colors."

"Damn!" cried the Advisor, who'd spoken up in defense of the Cabinet's youngest member. "There must be something to be done! That peach cobbler was truly beyond compare."

"If I may," offered another of the Elders. "Perhaps we are approaching the problem from the wrong direction. After all: we find ourselves in the ridiculous position of bargaining with a lowly Cook and his peasant brother."

"I agree," agreed the Secretary.

"I propose," continued the Elder, with a withering glance at the Secretary, "that we simply attempt to replace the *Cook*, rather than the cow, for a cow with such rare abilities is certainly a unique occurrence, and not likely repeated in a single generation, while a peach cobbler, delicious as it may be, can certainly be replicated by any capable chef."

"Bravo," replied the Secretary, dropping the ledger to applaud.

The issue was put to a vote, and the motion passed by overwhelming majority. The question then arose as to what should be done with the Cook and his brother, as both would certainly take umbrage with the Cabinet's decision, and as it went without saying that anyone brash enough to withhold peach cobbler from the King himself over so trifling and trivial a matter obviously did not hold the Crown in high enough regard, and could not be trusted. It was therefore proposed that the Cook and his brother be placed in the Castle's custody, and held in the dungeon until such time as it was determined that they had learned the error of their ways, and no longer presented any threat. This motion, too, was put to a vote, and overwhelmingly passed, and it was only after the vote had been tallied and the meeting adjourned that Hassock, red in the face and gasping for breath, appeared at the chamber door.

"Good sirs!" cried Hassock. "I thank God that I have arrived before we have adjourned, for I have news of the most pressing urgency which the King will not hear, and without the consideration of which I fear the Kingdom will not much longer stand!"

"Silence," replied the Elder whose suggestion it was to replace the Cook. "We'll have none of your sensational antics here! This is a place of considered discourse, not a market in which any idiot may stand upon a box and shout his insane theories!"

"Please," replied Hassock, "it is a matter of the direst urgency. The King's life may be in danger!" and here he fell to his knees in supplication, so that only his head was visible above the tabletop, along with his arms and hands, which he clasped in a gesture of earnest entreaty.

"Poppycock!" replied the Elder. "You've already won the post of Most Trusted Advisor: if you insist on twisting this Cabinet's ear along with the King's, you'll find me at least an unwilling participant."

"The meeting has already been adjourned," said the Secretary, in a tone intended to assuage Hassock's desperate disappointment. "If you'd like, I will linger a bit longer, and you may tell me all that you wish to tell the Cabinet. I assure you, I will put it at the top of the ledger for our next meeting."

"But by then it may already be too late," replied Hassock, allowing his head to hang in defeat. Then, animated by sudden inspiration, he rose to his feet and cried, "Assure me, then, that you have at least discussed the obvious and pressing matter of the disease which is now running a fierce course through the village, and the unmentionable horror in the courtyard, which is certainly its cause?"

"Um," replied the Secretary, looking from one face to another and then, when no eye would meet his, down at the ledger on the table. "No, I'm afraid we did not find the time to discuss that issue, either. But, as I said, if you would tell me what it is you have in mind, I will make sure that at our next meeting - ,"

"Hang the next meeting!" cried Hassock, grasping the Secretary by the collars. "This must be discussed now, or else it may be too late!"

"Unhand him!" cried the Elder, and the other Advisors fell upon Hassock with a fury hardly befitting men of their learning and stature, and beat him quite mercilessly, until he lay senseless upon the floor. "Take him to the dungeon," directed the Elder. "We'll have no more of his wild talk: not at the next meeting, nor ever again!"

This declaration was met with a great cheer of support, and Hassock's limp body was lifted and carried down the many stairs to the lowest dungeon. Here he was handed over to a pair of guards who eventually, and between the two of them, located all of the appropriate paperwork. Then the Advisors took their leave, and the guards accepted the prisoner, and brought him to his cell, taking turns carrying him, as he was the first prisoner to be placed in their charge since their promotion to prisoner guards (as the guards on duty during the riot had been beaten to death by the escaping prisoners, and the remainder of the guards were at home nursing sores and complaining alternately of heat and cold), and the newness of the position made everything seem exciting and wonderful, and neither wanted to miss any chance the other had.

31.

At that Moment, the King and the Soothsayer....

At that moment, the King and the Soothsayer were sitting on the floor of the King's bedchamber, crouched low within a makeshift enclosure comprised of a sheet laid over two chairs, inhaling the vapors from a small pot bubbling between them, and tending the small fire burning beneath it.

"Tell me," said the Soothsayer, "what Your Majesty sees."

"I see a great bear," said the King, thinking very hard. "He is climbing a tree, but the tree has buttresses instead of branches. He is climbing to the top of the tree. He is there to find something. I can't see what he is trying to find."

"Very good," said the Soothsayer, adding something else to the pot. "Go on."

"Now he's at the top," said the King. "He was looking for the moon. Now he has it. Yes."

"Wonderful," replied the Soothsayer. "What is he doing with the moon?"

"He's balancing it on his nose," replied the King, beginning to giggle. "He's balancing it on his nose and throwing it up and catching it on his nose. It's really a wondrous thing to see. Now he's taking it in his mouth and climbing back down. The sky is dark because the moon is gone. All of the other animals are crying and running into things."

"Yes," said the Soothsayer, ladling some of the pot's contents out with a long wooden spoon and offering it to the King. "Drink this, Your Majesty. It will help Your Majesty to see what the bear does next."

"Yes," agreed the King, taking the potion and drinking it down. "Oh, now I see. The bear isn't a bear at all. He's a badger. No, wait. Now he's a lizard. Now I'm not sure what he is. All of the other animals are gathering around him, and they don't know what he is either. They're going to attack him! They're going to kill him!" and with this the King began to thrash wildly, as though defending the indeterminate animal against this attack, and in so doing overturned the pot and brought down the canopy, and caused the contents of the fire to be distributed beyond the tray on which they had been carefully arranged, and several holes were burned in the carpet and the bed sheet, and the guard on duty was called in to help stamp out the flames.

"Your Majesty," said the Soothsayer, when the excitement had passed, "I find it very interesting that you dreamt of a bear. Is there not a bear in Your Majesty's family crest? Perhaps Your Majesty is the bear in the vision. But then, what is the moon?"

"The moon is the moon," replied the King, standing at the open window and breathing in the fresh air, and shaking his head as though to rid it of the potion's effects. "Why must you speak in riddles? What should the moon be, but the moon?"

"Think, Majesty," replied the Soothsayer. "What did the bear do? He braved a hard and dangerous climb to achieve that which his heart most desired. What is it that Your Majesty most desires? What is it that Your

Majesty's Royalty and all of its attendant power has been unable to provide?"

"An heir!" cried the King, and fell instantly to weeping. "I would give my Crown and my life for a son to carry on my name!"

"Your Majesty is still very young," replied the Soothsayer, placing a comforting hand on the potentate's heaving shoulder. "There is no hurry! Your Majesty will reign for many years: I have seen this in a vision, and know it to be true. Your Majesty will be blessed with many sons, and they will rule as brothers, and have many sons of their own, and Your Majesty's name will live on for many generations!"

"But when?" cried the King. "How many more wives must I have before one gives me the child I desire? I swear by Heaven that I would bend myself to any extreme for her, if she could but give me that!"

"Careful Majesty!" replied the Soothsayer, "for recall the fate which befell the bear, when for the sake of the moon he changed himself into an unrecognizable form. Such may befall any man, and must surely befall a King who does not stand like the immobile and changeless Castle walls themselves!"

"Your wisdom is truly beyond compare," replied the King. "Here, consider this bedchamber: you must take from me any treasure contained herein, any you desire, for such is the depth and weight of my gratitude."

"The only treasure I desire," replied the Soothsayer, "is Your Majesty's health and happiness. But if Your Majesty insists that some gift must be given in gratitude, let it be only a lock of Your Majesty's hair, for I will take great satisfaction and comfort in knowing that a part of Your Majesty is forever with me, and will accept nothing else, though I be punished for my refusal, and sent to the deepest dungeon, no more will I relent."

"Noble and loyal countryman, I shall not refuse you!" replied the King.   And, springing to his feet, he drew his dagger and cut from his head a small lock of hair, which he bound with a ribbon and presented to the Soothsayer with great bravado and gravitas, and which the Soothsayer received in kind.   Then the two parted company, and the King called the guard to inquire whether the guard had a sister, and the Soothsayer left the castle grounds, and headed in the direction of the Great Forest, clutching its prize tightly to its breast.

32.
Hazaiah's Reception, and What Followed

The band of warriors and peasants, whose number had been further diminished during the night by a fever (brought on, it was assumed, by the swamp water which they had for many days been forced by necessity to drink) which had claimed the lives of two of its members, and rendered two more unable to meet the summons of Hazaiah's emissary (which two, the village Doctor feared, would not likely last another day and night), made its way along the central avenue leading to Hazaiah's estate, showered with laurels and cries of welcome from the congregated townspeople. At the gate they were greeted by Hazaiah himself who, sitting atop a carriage carried by a half-dozen guardsmen in impressively gilded armor, bade them welcome and led them, with various directions, provocations, and rebukes to his couriers, up the steps and through the massive doors, and into the vast dining chamber in which a grand feast had been set.

"Welcome, welcome!" cried Hazaiah, gesturing broadly and spilling from the goblet he carried a great quantity of wine, which splashed on the heads of those bearing him aloft. "You are guests in my home, and I am most honored to receive you. Eat, drink, and make yourselves comfortable. My humble estate is yours for as long as you require."

"Thank you," replied the warrior who was now in the lead, whose name was Herarites. "We are grateful for your hospitality, and are in your debt."

"Oh, pish posh," answered Hazaiah.

At this moment one of the guardsmen, succumbing to both the weight of his ornate armor and his portly charge, collapsed, causing the entire assembly to topple and deposit its noble cargo in a graceless heap upon the flagstones.

"Sire!" shouted the guardsmen, in great panic and embarrassment, but also with considerable confusion, for it was obvious from their groping and crawling that they could see little through their beautiful visors.

"Oh, my head!" cried Hazaiah, clutching at his scalp, from which there issued a disturbingly prodigious stream of blood. "I am killed! You idiots have killed me! Oh God, take pity on your humble servant!"

"Now!" cried Herarites, and he drew his sword and fell upon the nearest guardsman, and stabbed him repeatedly through the joints in his armor, while the guardsman fumbled for his own weapon.

"You fool!" cried one of the other warriors, whose name was Hororro. "You'll bring the entire army down upon us!"

"It's too late to argue about it," put in the third and, as circumstances stood, only other warrior in the greatly diminished group. And here he drew his own sword and set about dispatching the remaining guardsmen with startling speed and ferocity.

"Guards, guards!" cried Hazaiah, still clutching at his wounded head. "Help me, we are betrayed!" and here he crawled beneath the nearest of the great banquet tables and cowered behind a chair which, though substantial, did little to hide his considerable bulk.

"You lot, bar the door," said the third warrior, whose name was Hurahura, pointing the peasants toward the main door, which still stood open wide. "And when you've finished with that, bar any door you can find leading off this chamber."

"You incomparable idiot," said the second warrior to the first, striking him with the flat of his sword. "You've sealed our fate with your rashness!"

"Do not trifle with me," replied the first, brandishing his own blade. "I'll spill your blood as quickly as I spilled theirs."

"Both of you, stop your bickering," interrupted Hurahura, stepping between them. "What's done is done: we're in it now, and there's no use arguing how it came about. Go and make sure that no one else can get in, and then we will discuss what is to be done."

"Who put you in charge?" replied Herarites, turning to menace Hurahura with his blade. "The prize is mine, I claimed my chance: you will court my favor as the others do, or feel my steel!"

"I see," said Hurahura, and in a single deft movement diverted the sword-tip hovering near his face and plunged his dagger into Herarites' heart. Herarites, gasping in pain and surprise, clutched somewhat awkwardly at Hurahura's face, then fell to the floor. Hurahura, removing the blade, turned his attention to Hororro and said, "Shall we quarrel for leadership, or do you reason, as I do, that such dire circumstances as those in which we find ourselves require a more cooperative strategy?"

"I stand with you," replied Hororro. "What more is there for a reasonable man to do, when nature and fate have conspired against him? Though dimwitted enough to begin this misbegotten quest, I do not lack the wit to see that we will survive together, or not at all."

"Very good," replied Hurahura, sheathing both sword and dagger. "Have the doors been sealed?"

"As best as can be hoped," replied one of the peasants, chewing on a morsel from the over-stocked tables. "Which is to say that they're as blocked up as they're going to be, but there's no locks on any of them, and we haven't the keys to lock them anyway."

"How can you eat at a time like this?" asked another of the peasants, considering the first with an odd mix of disbelief and annoyance. "Haven't we got bigger concerns?"

"Well," replied the first, but his explanation was here interrupted by an arrow which passed into his open mouth and through the back of his neck.

"Archers!" cried Hurahura, "seek cover!" and dove beneath the nearest table as a dozen arrows struck the flagstones in the place he had been standing.

"This is certainly a fantastic mess," said Hororro, pushing chairs out of the way to hunker down beside Hurahura, and from here considered the second-story balcony overlooking and encircling the dining hall, where what appeared to be the entire archery corps stood ready to let fly. "We're cooked, there's no doubt about it. Curse that damned Herarites!"

"No use cursing him now," replied Hurahura, shouting over the drumming of arrows into the wood above their heads. "Better use your time now to think of a plan or say your prayers, for little else will profit you as much in this life or the next. How have the peasants fared?"

"Much worse than us, I fear, replied Hororro. "That first one was dead before he hit the floor, and of the others I see that at least one has gone to his reward. Two are under that far table, but one appears to be shot through, and I see another hiding in that corner there, with an arrow in his foot."

"I don't understand!" wailed Hazaiah, still clutching at his bleeding skull. "I offer you food and drink! I welcome you into my home! The Devil holds secret torments for he who so flagrantly and so vilely betrays hospitality!"

"Shut your flapping jowls," replied Hurahura. And, drawing his dagger, he placed the still-bloodied tip against the fat man's undulating throat and said, "Tell those archers to stop shooting at us."

"Archers!" cried Hazaiah, his voice grown shrill and frantic at the sight of the blade, "Cease what you are doing at once!"

"Now tell them to bring three horses around to the front door," said Hororro, peeking out from beneath the table in the sudden silence that followed Hazaiah's command.

"For the love of God!" cried Hazaiah, beginning to cry and whimper, "Bring three horses to the front door!"

"What about us?" asked the peasant beneath the table opposite, who had not been hurt, but who held close beside him the peasant who had been shot through, and from whose mouth there issued a great profusion of blood. "You can't just leave us here!"

"And me as well!" cried the peasant from whose foot an arrow protruded.

"Silence, everyone!" shouted Hurahura, his own voice growing somewhat strained and shrill. "Where is the Captain of the Archers? Who is in command?"

"I am," replied the Captain of the Archers, leaning slightly over the railing. "Please know that we have you entirely surrounded. Further, you should be aware that there are fifty more men posted about the manor's exterior, with bows strung and arrows at the ready. Should you make any attempt to escape, I assure you that these men will cut you down without the slightest difficulty."

"It seems you have us at somewhat of a disadvantage," replied Hurahura.

"I should say so," replied the Captain of the Archers.

"Perhaps we can talk this through," offered Hurahura.

"I don't think that's very likely," replied the Captain.

"We do have your Lord under here, you know," offered Hurahura.

"Yes, that's true," replied the Captain, considering. "But you have to realize that by killing him, you would only assure your own demise. Better to let him go, and hope that he is kind enough to repay the favor with a show of mercy."

"Such hope seems ill-founded," replied Hurahura, "when the party in question is one so notorious that the King himself demands his head."

"The King?" said Hazaiah, so startled by this revelation that for a moment his voice lost its frantic edge. "Why on earth would the King call for my head? I've done nothing to Him! I've done everything in my power to serve as an honest and loyal vassal not only to His rule, but also to that of His father! My God! Do we live in such a world that honesty and kindness are thusly repaid?"

"Never mind that," said Hurahura, giving the bulge of fat beneath Hazaiah's chin an unfriendly poke with his dagger. "The reasoning behind the King's request is neither our business nor our concern. He made the request and offered the reward: His reasons are His own."

"My God!" cried Hazaiah, falling so completely into uncontrollable sobs that he neglected even to clasp at the still-bleeding wound atop his head. "Are lives so cheap? Does my head as it is now, and by this I mean upon my body, merit so little consideration that it may be bartered like a piece of fruit at the market? What horror it is to see oneself become a Thing, divested of all human substance and worth!"

"Your position is untenable," cut in the Captain of the Archers, interrupting the thread of Hazaiah's lamentations. "Release your prisoner, and I give my word you will be given a fair trial under the law."

At this moment there came from without the sound of three horses whinnying in protest of some unknown injury or injustice.

"Tell your archers to lower their bows," countered Hurahura, "and I give you my word that not one drop of your overfed Lord's blood will be spilled until he is allowed to stand before the King and hear the complaint leveled against him."

"Very clever," replied the Captain of the Archers. "So it is put to me that I must either follow the King's order, and allow my Lord to be taken by force, or stand against the King and make an enemy of the Crown. Truly a conundrum! But of course, these stakes stand only so long as I trust your word, and you must forgive me if I am remiss to do so. The claim that you and your companions are in earnest, and honest and true, if I am to judge from your actions thus far, strains credulity. No, I think it is far better to kill you here, and let the King speak in his own voice if we have acted against Him. Then, at least, we will know the truth of the matter."

"Very well," replied Hurahura, and with a great lunge and a pull emerged from beneath the table with Hazaiah before him like a shield, the dagger's point still prodding the fat man's pudgy neck. "If you wish to shoot me, you must do so through your beloved Lord!"

"Not hardly," replied the Captain of the Archers, "for you see the balcony of this striking chamber runs the full perimeter, and thus you will observe that there are archers both before and behind. We may shoot you with ease, no matter which direction you face."

"A very troubling dilemma," replied Hurahura, "but one for which I am not wholly unprepared." And here, dropping the dagger, he hoisted the prisoner onto his shoulders so that Hazaiah's considerable backside was topmost and his red and sweating face hung down in the perfect image of humiliation and shame. So substantial was Hazaiah's bulk, and so high and narrow the hall, and so positioned was the balcony that the archers above could find no angle from which to fire, and so fell to tumbling over each other in their search for an effective vantage.

"Stop it, stop it!" cried the Captain of the Archers, "I command you to stop at once!"

"Stop them!" cried Hazaiah, wheezing quite a bit and waving his arms, though the latter motion seemed to exhaust him, and he stopped as quickly as he had begun.

During this commotion Hurahura, grunting and straining and staggering beneath his load, proceeded a half-dozen paces to the door. Here, however, his overtaxed legs failed him, and he dropped to a knee, and seemed quite incapable of any further progress. He was saved, however, by Hororro, who hurried from beneath the table and took up Hazaiah's legs. Bearing their prize they exited the hall, grunting and straining and staggering together, and entirely ignoring the cries of the peasants who they had left behind. Once outside, and with great effort and ingenuity, they set Hazaiah (who was now sobbing unreservedly, and making pleas to God, and also offering his assailants various gifts should his life be spared) atop his horse, and mounted their own, and set off in a frantic gallop, though their horses veered badly from side to side, as each had been given a grievous wound to one of its legs, and proceeded forward in great pain, and ran as though by doing so it might outpace or outmaneuver the effects of its affliction. No sooner had their flight begun than they were at once engulfed in a great volley of arrows, and all three were struck, and Hazaiah slumped from his horse, though perhaps more from despair than the effects of his injury, which was discovered to be minor when his captors dismounted and assisted him, themselves bleeding from their newly-received wounds, during which efforts one of the horses ran away, and after which the warriors were obligated to ride together, leading their still inconsolable prisoner, as further volleys pursued them, until they were quite out of range.

"What injustice it is to be a man!" cried Hazaiah to the indifferent fields through which they rode, and to the indifferent clouds beneath which they rode, and to the blue and endless and insensate heavens. "What sore hardship I am heir to! Why does God see fit to punish me thusly? I am ever a loyal and faithful and pious servant! I am as inoffensive as any man of my rank, which is to say I am no more offensive than any of my equals! Surely I am deserving of some consideration or mercy!"

At that moment Hazaiah's horse, startled by a bird which flew unexpectedly from the high grass through which they rode, reared and threw Hazaiah. The portly vassal, clutching at the wound he had received in the first volley, which was low on his back and in an awkward place to reach, was ill-positioned to brace for such a fall and so toppled end over end, and landed precisely on his head, which as bad luck would have it struck a large and rather pointy rock, and broke open like a melon, and spilled its contents onto the loam. The horse, not bothering to consider the fate of its passenger, and still apparently frightened by the bird's unexpected flight, took off at a great pace.

"Great God!" cried Hurahura, and reined in his own horse, and brought it around, and in so doing caused Hororro to slip from the saddle, and fall to the ground, and reveal by the posture he there assumed the great quantity of blood coating his torso and soaking his garments, and the arrow-point protruding from his belly, where the arrow had passed through his body.

"Help me!" cried Hororro, writhing in the dirt. "Friend Hurahura, I fear they have killed me."

"Oh, ho!" replied Hurahura, not bothering to dismount, but speaking down to Hororro from atop his charger. "Indeed, you seem in a very sorry state; it pains me terribly to leave you this way, but, as you obviously require more care than I am able to provide, and as we have only one horse, and as I have no more need for your aid in managing our prisoner's bulk, I'm afraid I must."

Then, laughing somewhat hysterically, he dismounted and cut Hazaiah's head from his body, a task which took a terribly long time, for the fat about the corpse's neck had grown quite solid and rigid, and the body could not be easily moved for more advantageous positioning. While he was doing this the sun fell and hovered beside the horizon, and Hororro moaned and whimpered, and made pleas to God, and also offered Hurahura various gifts should his life be saved. But finally these pleas and entreaties ceased, and the last tendon was severed, and Hurahura gathered his prize and rode what little distance he was able in the rapidly-ebbing daylight, and made camp, and sat considering the somewhat stunned expression on the face of the head in his hands, and wondering also how long it would take him to return to the Kingdom, and thinking of what he would do with his riches once he returned there, and all of the things he would enjoy in his new and wonderful life.

Later that night the peasant who had not been injured, whose name was Hewthew (and who had escaped the manor and its environs only by the skin of his teeth, first running frantically to avoid the falling arrows, then stowing himself in barns and amidst flocks of sheep when the Captains of the Guard began their search, and finally hiding amidst reeds in water up to his nose when the dogs came), and who had traveled the many miles on foot in pursuit of the warriors and their prize, fell upon the sleeping Hurahura and beat his skull in with a crude club he had fashioned from a felled branch. Then, taking both head and horse, he continued west through the forest until the ground beneath the horse's feet grew soft, and the air hung heavy with the smell of rot and decay, and the calls of the night animals were frightening and unfamiliar. Here he paused, and as the morning sun crested the horizon offered a prayer to God, and asked that he be given safe passage through the swamp and across the lake on the other side, and also through the forest beyond, and all the way back to the Castle, where his reward awaited him. Then he mounted the horse and entered the swamp, and after some little distance the horse's hooves became mired in the unreliable ground, and the horse could proceed no further, and began in fact to sink, and Hewthew dismounted and considered his dilemma, and cursed his luck, and attempted to construct various apparatuses by which he might extricate the beleaguered beast, each of which failed to produce any meaningful effect, and during which time the horse sank lower and lower, whinnying and thrashing as best it could as the water and mud closed in about it.

Soon only the horse's head remained visible, and Hewthew petted its ears, and spoke to it, and assured it that it would be received in Heaven, but also wept uncontrollably, and had to turn away when the animal finally disappeared beneath the surface. Then, gathering the head (and brushing from it the various insects that had, as he sat speaking to the horse, taken up residence along its surface, and in its various orifices, and also in its hair), he continued westward, repeating to himself the assurance that God would not have allowed him to come so far only to abandon him now, that despite all hardship and travail he need not be afraid, for all was certainly part of His plan.

33.
The Doctor's Plan for Containment and Recovery

"Your Majesty," began the Doctor, when all assembled had been seated, and the Secretary of the Council of Advisors had indicated with a nod that the floor was now his. "We have a most dire situation on our hands. While some would wile away the hours with talk of blame and fault, and who should have done what, and whose responsibility it is, I am like Your Majesty a man of action, and ill-contented with long hours spend in decision-less speculation. I will therefore, if it pleases Your Majesty, dispense with all consideration of the cause or causes of this crisis, and move immediately into a meditation on what is to be done about the situation in which we find ourselves."

"Naturally," replied the King, looking about as though he was not quite certain which crisis the Doctor was referring to, or its exact nature, and so was hoping to discover in the faces of the Advisors some clue as to the appropriate response. "Of course. Carry on."

"We are, as Your Majesty is no doubt aware, experiencing something of a medical anomaly," the Doctor went on. "It is not often that one is given the opportunity to consider and study a disease at the moment of its genesis. Which is to say: I can find no history of an illness with the progressive symptoms unique to the one which we now observe ravaging the village beyond the Castle's walls, and I am therefore inclined to conclude that nothing of its kind has ever existed before."

"I see," said the King, looking around for the Page bearing the wine jug, as he had emptied his cup during the Doctor's preamble. "Please, continue."

"Very good," said the Doctor, and made a gesture through the open door, in response to which entered a phalanx of paired guards, each bearing between them a peasant in one of the stages of the disease's progress, several of whom could not stand under their own power, and had to be carried. There here followed some confusion, as the stages of the disease had become scrambled in the hallway, and had to be put back in order, a task for which the Doctor was only somewhat prepared, having become only recently acquainted with this malady's particular progress, and having as of yet failed to find adequate time to conduct an exhaustive study, being somewhat distracted by the many pleasures and diversions afforded by his newfound status and wealth.

"As Your Majesty can plainly see," said the Doctor, once the rearranging was complete, and the peasants stood (or were held) in something very near the correct order, "the illness starts rather innocently. Its victim will experience these small red and black blisters that, though sensitive to the touch, hardly pose an encumbrance." Here he poked at one of the many sores encircling the first peasant's ankles, a move which produced both a sharp yelp from the peasant himself and a fresh profusion of blood from the wound. "Moving on," the Doctor continued, moving down the line, "as Your Majesty can see, the disease makes itself known over the next several days by conquest and expansion: the sores spread and grow larger, and as they do the peasant finds himself increasingly fatigued. His condition is here characterized by a loss of appetite and a general and pervasive malaise. He thinks only of his bed, but when he is there he finds no relief, for the sores forming all over his body pain and irk him. By the fifth day," the Doctor said, stepping now in front of the fifth patient, who seemed to be in great pain, and could not stand but was held on his feet by the attendant guardsmen, "the peasant undergoes a profound and debilitating change, coughing and vomiting uncontrollably and experiencing fever and chills." Here, as though on cue from the Doctor, the peasant fell into a violent coughing fit which ended with him vomiting onto the floor. "Finally," said the Doctor, stepping around the mess, "we come to the third and final stage of the disease: the patient, though now covered in lesions and unable to stand, feels no pain at all."

"Honestly," said the patient, who was held aloft by a pair of guards. "I feel fine."

"This, unfortunately," said the Doctor, "is not an indication of the disease's remission, but is rather its final ironic act. It takes only the slightest pressure," and here the Doctor prodded one of the patient's lesions with his finger, at which provocation the lesion broke open and released a foul smell and a great quantity of blood, "to set the patient on the path to destruction."

All watched with fascination as, for the next several minutes, this final patient shifted with increasingly violent and frantic gestures in the guards' arms: each movement caused another lesion to burst, and the guards and the floor about them was soon covered in blood, and all the air in the room befouled by the smell, and the patient screamed and begged for someone to murder him, and the other patients looked on with horror, and considered their own lesions, and some of them wept openly, and begged God for mercy, and also offered the Doctor all that they had if only he would cure them. Finally the cries ceased, and the peasant lay still, and the guards begged permission to go and wash up, and the King rose from his throne and applauded, being rather impressed with the presentation.

"But what is to be done?" asked one of the Advisors, once the guards and peasants had left the room, and the floor mopped, and the windows opened to let out the lingering stench.

"The disease is highly contagious," replied the Doctor. "I therefore think it best that, as an immediate and preliminary measure, all peasants be disallowed access to the Castle. This includes, I'm afraid, banning them from Sunday market, which I know is a great favorite amongst the lower castes. Unfortunately, such dire circumstances call for extreme measures."

"Very well," replied the Most Trusted Advisor, a man named Hufdeefee, who had been elected to the post in Hassock's absence. "What else?"

"I think it is in the best interest of all involved," the Doctor went on, somewhat tentatively, "that a second wall be constructed between the village and the Castle. It has occurred to me that as the peasants discover not only that they are doomed to such hideous suffering, but also that they have been denied access to the Castle, which we must hold as a bastion of health, they may attempt some sort of assault which, though holding a laughable probability of success, may succeed insofar as those recruited to quell the attack will come in close contact with the diseased, and may become infected. A second wall will allow our archers to fire down upon them from a distance across which the disease cannot travel."

"Also an excellent suggestion," replied the Most Trusted Advisor. "Please, continue."

"Beyond these minor suggestions," replied the Doctor, "I can offer only that I am in the midst of an exhaustive study on the exact cause and nature of this vile affliction, and am making new and interesting discoveries on an almost hourly basis. I am confident that in very little time I will know of a treatment guaranteed to eliminate this disease once and for all."

"Very good," replied the Most Trusted Advisor.

"Just a quick point of clarification," said the Secretary. "You say that the disease is very contagious, contagious enough that any who come in passing contact with the infected in a fight might, themselves, become infected. How is it, then, that we are free from this danger? We, after all, have now all been in extremely close contact with some infected individuals."

"Yes," murmured the other Advisors, turning a rather scrutinous and somewhat unfriendly gaze upon the Doctor. "Please tell us why we should not be concerned."

"Why, good sirs," replied the Doctor, in a tone suggesting that the need to explain something so obvious and simple had never crossed his mind, "because the disease only afflicts the peasantry."

"Ah," replied the Advisors, breathing a collective sigh. "Of course."

Then, all laughing together at their moment of trepidation, they exited the chamber, pausing only briefly without to wipe from the soles of their shoes the blood that, not yet fully cleaned from the flagstones, had dirtied their heels.

34.

The Advancing Army Makes Its Presence Known, and What Followed

At precisely that moment there was a terrific crash, and the tower in which the King and the Advisors stood shook, and two of the Advisors were grievously wounded by falling debris, and another two struck but not very badly hurt, and the King himself sent into a coughing fit by the dust that drifted down, and several toes were stepped on and eyes poked in the confusion that resulted. The guardsmen, hurrying to the window, announced that an army bearing the flag and colors of Isthinrod had emerged from the woods, that they were launching boulders of incredible size from a variety of machines, that the village beyond the wall was already quite destroyed and ablaze and that the villagers, seeking shelter, were pouring into the courtyard.

"Majesty," said one of the Advisors who had been struck, pressing his hands to a rather large wound on his forehead (by which he accomplished very little, for the blood continued to flow rather freely), "I must insist that we shut the bridge against the peasants. If we leave it open for too long the enemy will surely make its way inside! Further, we must recall the good Doctor's advice. What would happen if the courtiers took ill?"

"I will not shut my gates on my people," replied the King, still coughing fitfully, and speaking with difficulty. "We've had the Doctor's word that the disease only afflicts the peasantry: we therefore have nothing to fear from their presence among us!"

Here there was another crash, and several more pieces of debris fell from the ceiling, and one of the Advisors who had been gravely injured was killed on the spot by a falling brick, and another two sorely injured, and the Most Trusted Advisor declared that the party should be moved to a more stable location, lest any further disaster befall them. The party then set off in a great hurry, with the King in front and the Advisors behind, the ones in back pushed against those in front, who pressed back into those behind, to keep from toppling into the King, or stepping on his heels.

"Hurry!" cried those in the rear, as another boulder struck the tower's exterior. "The tower will fall, and we'll all be killed!"

"There's nothing to fear," replied those in front, "for we've achieved the stairs!"

The party entered the stairwell, moving hurriedly amongst themselves but also carefully so as not to jostle or rush the King, who remained in the lead, and was hampered somewhat by his violent coughing.

"Please hurry, Your Majesty!" cried those in the back, congregating and becoming somewhat wedged in the narrow and spiraling stairwell.

At that moment a boulder launched by one of the invading army's new devices struck the tower with sufficient force, and at just such an angle, that a sizable hole was created halfway up the northern side. As a result, and shortly following this impact, the northern side of the tower, from the hole to the peak, collapsed, sending those unfortunate enough to be standing along that wall at that moment plummeting to their deaths.

Those remaining within, left with the problem of how to descend a stairwell that lacked one quarter of its steps (for the stairwell ran along the tower's outer wall, and had been equally damaged in the collapse), disregarded the King's wellbeing entirely and fell to executing all manner of panicked solutions, the most unsuccessful of which involved jumping through the vacancy to the battlement below, a distance of some dozen or so meters, the attempt of which produced no shortage of injuries and, in the case of one elderly Advisor, the almost complete shattering of the many bones of the lower extremities.

The King, being first among the descending party, and being somewhat ahead of the rest (who had become in fact nearly inexorably wedged in the narrow space in their hurry, and who were only dislodged by the projectile's impact, which both jarred them and reduced their number), descended the remainder of the intact stairwell and hurried through the Castle to the entrance of the dungeon where he stood for some time, listening carefully for any sound of further assault.

"Goodness," said one of the two guards on duty, noticing him. "Look there. It's the King."

"Nonsense," replied the second, hardly bothering to look up from the stick he was carving. "What on earth would the King be doing down in a place like this? The very thought is ridiculous. If I didn't know any better, I might say you're coming down with a touch of the Illness."

"I'm telling you," answered the first, a note of annoyance entering his voice, crossing his fingers twice and spitting on the floor as a safeguard against the

Illness, "it's the King Himself. I saw Him once, and I would swear to God Himself that it was Him."

"Well then," said the second, looking up with an air of indulgence, "let's have a look at your King." He stared hard down the hallway for several moments, considering the figure, before concluding loudly, "No. Can't be Him. The King is much taller. Besides, it can't be Him. What would He come down here for?"

"Think what you want," replied the first, "but I say it can't hurt to address Him as if He were the King, just in case. If I'm wrong, then I'm no worse for it. If I'm right, I may avoid the lash or the boot." Then, rising from his stool, he hailed the King and saluted in a grand display of military formality.

"Silence, you idiot," snapped the King, hardly bothering to look in the guard's direction.

"I told you," replied the second guard, laughing into his hat.

"No use, no use at all," murmured Hassock, leaning against the wall of his cell, regarding the proceedings with a disdainful and resigned air. "You can't get blood from a stone. Save your breath."

"And what do you know about it?" replied the guard, growing red in the face and slapping at his colleague's arm, in a vain attempt to quiet the other's laughter, a gesture which produced only a second explosive expression of mirth.

"Oh, I know quite a bit about it," replied Hassock, picking at the small red and black scabs forming on his arms and legs. "You wouldn't know it to look at me now, but I was once the King's Most Trusted Advisor. I slept on a feather mattress and had my pick of the Royal Courtesans. Not that I enjoyed it: I was too busy and nervous all the time, trying to get the King to listen. In the end, this is where it got me! I can tell you from experience: if you see the King coming, better to look the other way and pretend you never saw Him at all."

"Shut up, you," said the second guard, and hurled the stick he had been carving at Hassock. "One more word from you and I'll fix your wagon for good and all. No one cares what goes on down here: I could sort you out and no one would be the wiser."

"It would be just as well," replied the former Advisor. "Whether I last a day or a year, I know this room will be the last I see."

The King, meanwhile, had been moving steadily toward the speaker, and now addressed the prisoner. The guards stood to attention and saluted, and the second sharply rebuked the prisoner for failing to do so. The King, however, seemed indifferent to Hassock's lack of genuflection, and instead demanded that Hassock be released at once. Hassock, suspicious of the King, inquired why he should be released, to which the King replied that the Castle was under attack, and that he required Hassock's good judgement and council. Hassock, his elation tempered by his horror at news of the attack, rose to his feet and followed the King to the entrance of the dungeon, where he turned to spit and curse furiously at the guards, who bowed their heads and received his insults in the manner befitting the subservient classes. Crossing the courtyard they were puzzled by an inauspicious sound, like the roaring of a great wind, and overtaken by a sudden shadow, and had only time to inquire of each other what these signs might mean, when at once they were both buried beneath a great quantity of stone and timber, as the much-assaulted tower finally collapsed.

It was several hours before they were uncovered and, as the soldiers who remained were all required at their posts, much of the work was done by the Advisors (many of whom now exhibited severe limps and other injuries as evidence of their leap from the tower). The two were unburied together, the reinstated Advisor having received the lesser of the injuries, as he had been standing behind the King, and so had been buried beneath him, and was able to rise from the rubble largely unharmed. The King, however, had been quite grievously injured, and was hardly breathing, and was carried to the nearest enclosure, whereupon he immediately expired, muttering incomprehensible words and phrases whose meaning no one present was able to determine. The Advisors then fell to fighting amongst themselves as to what was to be done: all agreed that some subterfuge should be enacted whereby it would appear that the King had not died, at least until the impending war was resolved, though none could agree who should stand in for him. This argument lasted for several hours until, by some strange phenomenon, all present seemed to realize at once that Hassock, after all, was nearly the same height and build as the deceased Monarch, and bore a distinct resemblance to him, and would do quite nicely as a replacement until some other solution could be found.

And so it was settled: the (somewhat dented and bloodied) Crown was removed from the King's head and placed on Hassock's, and all knelt and pledged their allegiance, and the King's body was stripped of its finery and returned to the rubble, where (thus divested of telltale accouterment) all agreed he would go unrecognized, if and when he was discovered. Hassock, overwhelmed and elated, suppressed the cough he felt rising in his throat, and thanked them all for the honor, and pledged to rule the country well and decently until such a time came that his service was no longer required.

Thus united in their plot the assembly made its exit, moving slowly across the courtyard, as none save Hassock could walk without pain, and a few of the older Advisors had to be carried. Descending into the fortified War Room Hassock reflected what a strange turn of fortune he'd had, and how pleasant it was to be out of the dungeon, and also how he would certainly have to get the Doctor to take a look at the lesions forming on his legs and arms, as they troubled him greatly and caused him considerable pain, and seemed to bleed quite a lot at the slightest provocation.

35.
The Captain of the Archers, in Pursuit

When it became clear that Hazaiah's captors had crossed the border into the Mercurial Swamp (when every barn had been searched and every cart overturned, and also every house inspected and every foreigner questioned, and some imprisoned) the Captain of the Archers, being a man of honor, and being therefore greatly disgraced by the occurrences in the Dining Hall, begged the Council of Elders' leave to pursue Hazaiah's captors himself, with only a small accompaniment, so that he might right his failure and return the beloved vassal to his heartbroken people. The Council of Elders, however, had never been consulted on anything more pressing than the possible meaning of weather patterns, or the hidden and ominous significance of certain unexplained happenings, and therefore felt ill-equipped to render a verdict with such far-reaching implications and upon whose outcome so many relied. A broader council was therefore called for, and a number of landholders and peasants gathered, and a week lost in the process, during which the Captain of the Archers bit his tongue and sat on his hands, and thought ceaselessly of all that might befall his Lord. Finally this newly-convened council adjourned, and rendered its verdict, and granted leave to the Captain pending a secondary review, which would be undertaken no sooner than ten days but no longer than fourteen days after the Captain's departure, all of which seemed reasonable to - and was readily accepted by - the Captain, overanxious as he was to be off.

The search party left amidst great fanfare, and many kisses were blown and handkerchiefs given as tokens of affection, and a fatted calf was slaughtered, and also several goats, whose carcasses were burned in offering, and the Priest blessed the Captain and his efforts, and the party left the city and traveled into the country, and then progressed further into the forest whose westernmost edge bordered the Mercurial Swamp, entering it some miles north of the place where, seven days earlier, Hazaiah had been thrown from his horse and killed and where, despite the efforts of several hungry animals, the majority of his headless body remained.

The modest company included a soldier renowned for his tracking skills, another who was skilled in hand-to-hand combat, another who was known to climb trees and rock formations with great dexterity, and the Captain himself. It did not include, however, any man familiar with the Mercurial Swamp (such men were hard to come by in Hazaiah's lands, as the Mercurial Swamp was generally avoided and was considered by some to be haunted) and likewise upon entering the region the search party made slow progress, and lost several items in the muddy and murky quagmire, including an ornate dagger given to one of the soldiers (the one who climbed trees with great dexterity) by Hazaiah himself as a special reward for service and bravery, the loss of which pained the soldier greatly, and inspired bitter tears, and brought with it the specter of despair, for the soldier became convinced that such an omen boded ill for the entire endeavor, and for a time would continue no further, until he was placated by the others. Their supply of food was also heavily taxed, both moving forward and resting, for as they moved along the muddy and capricious ground various odds and ends shook loose and fell into the swamp, and were lost or soiled beyond edibility, and as they rested the many creatures who lived in the swamp burrowed into their store and ate of its contents. Soon there was insufficient food to sustain them, and they fell to foraging, and for a time forgot all about Hazaiah in their hunger. After an indeterminate interval (the light in the swamp was so poor that it was often difficult to tell night from day, and morning from evening) they awoke to a terrific crashing, which soon revealed itself to be a vast company of mounted cavalry which, on the direction of the council convened of peasants, landholders, and Elders, was marching west through the swamp in search and in support of the search party, of which nothing had been heard for some time.

"This is an unforgivable disgrace," wailed the Captain of the Archers, spilling from his mouth a great quantity of crumbs, for his sorrow had not lessened his hunger, and he ate with great voraciousness of the bread offered to him by the Officer leading the Cavalry.

"Calm yourself," replied the Officer, "and cease your weeping! Your womanly lamentations do little to secure the return of our beloved Lord."

"I fear that I have already doomed him by my failure," moaned the Captain, coughing somewhat as in speaking he began to choke on the bread in his mouth. "I fear that our Lord has met some terrible end!"

"Whether he has or has not is utterly irrelevant," answered the Officer. "Our task is to pursue his captors, and to do so with unending ardor. To do any less would be a disservice to either our Lord or, if he has perished, his memory."

"But certainly we are no better for your company than we were on our own," replied the Captain, "for the work of many is no better than the work of few, when all must work as one and the way is unclear. Or have you found some means of negotiating this damned and interminable quagmire?"

"We have not," admitted the Officer, "though such troubles me less than I imagine it has troubled you these fourteen days, for we have secured the services of a Seer whose vision far surpasses that which is commonly granted by God to mortal man." And here, turning about, the Officer gave a great wave and shouted, "Mage, come forward! Show yourself and be known!"

A hooded figure, riding atop a sickly red-eyed mount, emerged from the congregation and made its way to where the Captain and the Officer sat conversing. The Captain, hungry as he was, stopped eating, and the Officer involuntarily recoiled. The rider, removing its hood, stroked the few whiskers which dangled from its chin and considered the men with broad, unblinking eyes.

"Seer," said the Officer, forcing himself to resume his natural posture, "you have led us faithfully to the men we sought; now tell us in which direction we should continue, as all among us are eager to find and reclaim our beloved Lord, be he alive or dead."

"Yes," replied the Seer, still stroking its whiskers. "You are noble men, and so wish only to continue upon your noble quest! But the answers you seek, I fear, lie far from nobility!" and here the Mage drew from its bag a large black bird which flapped its wings and cried out in a coarse and bleating tone and from which both the Captain and the Officer recoiled in terror. Gripping the bird by the wings the Soothsayer gave a great cry and a pull, and a terrible crackling was heard, and the bird's tone grew shrill, and the wings were torn from the body, and the immobile body fell lifeless upon the ground, and sank into the inconstant mud, and the wings continued to flap and fold, and the Soothsayer fought them with great effort, until finally their motions ceased and they hung lifeless and still.

"Good God!" cried the Officer in charge of the Cavalry, while beside him the Captain of the Archers vomited up the bread he had only just finished eating.

"There now," said the Soothsayer, wholly unperturbed by their display. "The body has disappeared: such bodes well for your quest! A visible lifeless body would mean that the man you seek has perished; the absence of a lifeless body indicates the presence of a living body. As for the wings, you see that they have come to rest with the tips pointing towards each other: such indicates that the way forward lies directly ahead. As for the blood: a great quantity would mean that a vast distance remains between you and your prize; as you can see, very little blood was spilled, and as such it is safe to say that you are nearing the end of your quest!"

"Well," said the Officer, heartened by this assessment and yet obviously disturbed by the process of its discovery, "very good. A token for your service," and here he handed the Soothsayer a leather purse which sounded with the clinking of the coins it contained.

"Thank you," replied the Seer, quickly pocketing the purse. And here, casting the wings to the ground, the figure returned its hood to its head and made again for the ranks of the assembled, and was soon lost among them.

"You have made a pact with the Devil Himself!" cried the Captain, when the Conjurer had gone. "God does not smile on such methods, no matter how necessary they seem! I fear in my soul that you have endangered not only our Lord but ourselves as well, by your reckless and blasphemous allegiances!"

"Quiet yourself," answered the Officer, "and do not forget that it was only by the Wizard's guidance that your sorry band was discovered. Further, do not presume any right to question my methods, you who have eaten of my bread, and who are indebted to my command that the Soothsayer discover your location before our Lord's!"

"Forgive me," replied the Captain, bowing his head. "You are correct: I owe you my life! It is only that I am greatly disturbed by the spectacle I have just witnessed, and needed a moment to collect my wits."

"Understandable," agreed the Officer. Then, digging into his pack, he retrieved a second, somewhat smaller loaf of bread and handed it across to the Captain, who received it with gratitude and ate of it with terrific appetite. Together they then brought the men to attention and, following the Soothsayer's instructions, continued forward with great gusto. After several hours they came to a broad expanse of standing water into which the men riding in front sank and quickly vanished. The Officer called for the men to halt and summoned the Soothsayer, who after an hour of searching still could not be found. Camp was made, and various options considered, and in the morning they fell to constructing a bridge by which the waterway could be crossed.

The bridge took several days to complete, and collapsed under the weight of the first to attempt it. Witnessing this failure the entire assembly fell into a profound despair from which it would not be roused, despite the Captain and the Officer's combined efforts. The Captain and the Officer, therefore, continued forward together, and soon discovered that some miles north the water could be easily and safely forded. When they returned, however, they found that in their absence the men had fallen to fighting amongst themselves, as food was growing scarce, and none wished to forage while others ate of stored provisions. Accordingly several men had been killed, and several others severely wounded, and the number of able-bodied men reduced nearly by half. The question then fell to the Captain and the Officer as to what should be done, for there was significant debate, as some felt that those who were wounded should be left behind, and should not be allowed to impede the progress of those who were not, while others felt that the wounded should be carried along, that it was inhuman to leave them behind, while still others felt that no further forward effort should be made, that the wounded should be tended to and nursed to health, at which time the entire assembly might proceed together. These three factions, each extolling the wisdom of its view, so taxed the ears of the Captain and the Officer that finally these commanding parties relinquished their authority and declared that every man was free to pursue his own end. This, however, produced further discussion, as none wished to be left to tend the wounded, for fear that he alone would be left to the duty. Nor did any wish to carry the wounded, and so it was finally decided by each man that he would go forward, and leave the wounded to their fate, and think no more upon it, and ignore the cries and pleas of those he left behind him.

"Horrible," said the Captain of the Archers. "What must God think of such monsters as we have become, to turn our backs on our brothers in so cruel and so cold a fashion?"

"Better not to consider it," agreed the Officer in charge of the Cavalry, casting a final glance in the direction of the camp. "We've more pressing concerns, at any rate, and might better put our thoughts to the health and wellbeing of those men in our charge than those whose plight God alone can alter."

They progressed some dozen or so miles, and came to the foot of a high ridge, and mounting it found the ground solid and the sun plainly visible, and also found innumerable forms of familiar vegetation, and also that the trees were free from the rot and hanging fungi and strange aberratious growths that were the hallmark of those of their brethren forced to grow in the dim twilight and unclean waters of the Mercurial Swamp. The entire assembly here fell to rejoicing, and congratulating one another, and wine that was being saved was opened and drunk, and a great many apologies and pardons given, for amongst the men there were many who held grudges against their compatriots for insults levied or blows received in the swamp, when food was scarce and tempers flared. Then, descending the slope, they came upon the encampment wherein the assembled peasants and warriors, working both day and night, had repaired their damaged ship and had (until recently) been awaiting (with lessening patience) the return of the small band sent to collect that which the King had demanded.

36.
To Which, in Response...

At this band's arrival the peasant Hewthew, who had arrived only a few hours earlier, and who bore the now somewhat decomposed (and, truth be told, foul-smelling) head in a sack which he had fashioned from his shirt, rose and hurried aboard the ship. Making his way to the lowest part of the hold he hid the head behind a pile of boxes and returned to shore, skirting the newly-arrived band and the Captain of the Archers in particular. His actions, however, did not go unobserved, and presently a great shout arose from the ship's deck, and all turned to see yet another peasant (a barrel maker, whose name no one had bothered to learn) dancing upon the railing and holding the head aloft, and declaring to all that he had claimed the head and so would win the prize. In reply the Captain of the Archers (horrified by the revelation that his master had perished, and likewise forgoing prudence in the name of vengeance) notched an arrow and fired it through the barrel maker's heart. The barrel maker, killed in the instant, released the head, which fell over the railing and onto the sand below.

There ensued a terrific struggle, and the peasants and warriors fell upon one another, as each attempted to claim the head for his own, while the Captain of the Archers and the Officer in charge of the Cavalry led their men in a heroic charge, riding into the midst of this melee and cutting down peasant and warrior alike, in the midst of which the head was further damaged, as great chunks of hair were pulled from its scalp and great gashes left in its cheeks and forehead by inadvertent blows. Finally the Captain of the Archers was pulled from his mount by a group of peasants and beaten (as they had no weapons, being only peasants) to bloody death; the Officer in charge of the Cavalry, observing that the tide had turned, called for retreat; the peasants and warriors (there remained only a few dozen), being exhausted from the battle, sought to resolve their dispute by diplomatic terms, and it was eventually decided (after several hours of heated debate) that all should claim the prize, and all should share equally in the reward, as no man was more deserving, after so many arduous trials, than any other.

The head (which, owing to its mutilations, had become almost unrecognizable, and had as well begun to render forth the larvae of insects whose eggs had been laid within its orifices and under its skin) was therefore placed in a new sack, and bound to the mast at such a height that no man, working alone, could hope to reach it. Then the entire assembly, working in unison, launched the vessel with the tide, and set sail, each man praying that no storm would arise and that no further trial awaited him, for each was weary to his soul and longed only for home and its promise of peace.

37.

The Commander of the Invading Force Demands an Audience

At the same moment that the ship set sail upon the Infinite Lake, an Emissary from the Isthinrod army was received through the somewhat damaged but still functional Castle gates; crossing the courtyard he regarded with revulsion the rank pile still moldering there, skirted the rubble of the collapsed tower (giving only a passing and indifferent glance to the body of the disrobed and thus unrecognizable King), and entered the ornate foyer wherein Hassock, fidgeting upon the throne, welcomed him with all the formality of seated Royalty.

"Your Majesty," cried the Emissary, unfurling a vast scroll and reading from it, "General Isoriso, Commander of the Isthinrod Army, leader of a force vast beyond comprehension, holder of those weapons before which Castle walls cannot stand and even Kings tremble, demands an audience with Your Worship to negotiate the terms of Your Majesty's surrender."

"My surrender?" replied Hassock, paying attention only at the utterance of this final phrase, as the innumerable sores on his arms and legs pained him terribly, and it took nearly all of his energy to keep from regarding them. "Your Commander wishes for my surrender?"

"That is the matter he wishes to discuss with Your Majesty," replied the Emissary. "What shall I tell him?"

"Great goodness," replied Hassock. "That's quite a tremendous thing. Certainly I will see him at once."

"What are you doing?" hissed the assembled Advisors, who came limping into the hall when the Emissary had gone. "You will discuss the terms of surrender with an invading General? Has your tenure in the dungeon robbed you of your senses?"

"It seems to me," replied Hassock, rolling up his sleeves and beginning to scratch with great ardor at his sores, "that at the very least no further attack will come while the Commander stands beneath our roof. Further, and I don't want to say I told you so, but it is an irrefutable fact that our force is woefully inadequate to drive away any invading army, as the vast majority of our fighting men have abandoned us to seek their prize. Perhaps surrender should not be so readily dismissed!"

"Silence," replied the new Most Trusted Advisor, a man named Heefeeheefee, who rose to that prestigious rank when the former Most Trusted Advisor succumbed, a few hours earlier, to wounds he received in his leap from the tower. "You dishonor the Crown and the King who wore it! Holy God in Heaven Himself bestowed these lands upon the King's father's father's father! It is a gesture not befitting either the King or his proxy, that those lands be given over to the first invader who demands them!"

"And yet I must again insist," replied Hassock, unable to suppress a smile, for he in fact very much enjoyed the debate and argument that accompanied the role of Advisor, and had missed it terribly during his imprisonment, "that a refusal to do so will result in further casualties, and very likely cause further and grievous damage to this, the King's ancestral home!"

This last remark, being in the vein of reverence for the King's lineage and landholdings, prompted consideration amongst the Advisors, and it was soon posited by some that the best course (the one showing the most regard for the King's memory) was indeed surrender, for it was (proponents of this view felt) only through surrender that the Castle's warders could attain guarantees of its preservation. This view was loudly and vehemently decried by Heefeeheefee, who took righteous offense at any suggestion that the Kingdom (having been granted to the King's father's father's father by God Himself!) pass into the hands of any not belonging to the King's bloodline, disregarding in his vehemence the well-known and often-bemoaned fact that the King had no heir to whom these lands might proceed. His diatribe, however, came to little, as his vote (though it counted double) was insufficient to outweigh the opinion shared by the others: that upon the Commander's entry into the Hall Hassock should bow and present, as a token of surrender, the finest of the King's scepters.

"Blasphemers, the entire lot of you!" cried Heefeeheefee, blinking back tears.

"Compel your lips to cease their flapping," advised another of the Advisors, "or we'll have someone see to it for you!"

At that moment a trumpet blast heralded the arrival of the Commander who, flanked by a half-dozen soldiers, entered the hall waving his saber above his head in such a gross display of warlike irreverence that Heefeeheefee was compelled to turn away in disgust. Hassock rose from the throne and offered the scepter; the Commander received it and considered it briefly; the soldier to whom it was passed, owing to the clumsiness of his gauntleted fingers, unceremoniously dropped it; Heefeeheefee bit his lip and said nothing, though further tears rose to his eyes.

"Then all that remains to be discussed," offered Hassock, "are the terms of your occupation."

"I fail to see how you are in any position to demand terms," replied the Commander, "as you have already made plain your intention to turn over your Castle and lands to Isthinrod. Nor does it seem that you are in possession of sufficient military strength to force terms upon us, for by my estimation a full assault by our force would produce, in less than a week's time, this same result. In short, an unconditional surrender seems your only option, and accordingly is the only one which we will accept."

"Monsters!" cried Heefeeheefee, unable to contain himself any longer. "Blasphemers, heathens, irreverent barbarians!" and here he drew from his robe a dagger with which he fell upon the nearest soldier, killing him in the instant.

The Commander, falling behind the others, took up again the scepter and began to swing it wildly, as to strike down any advancing foe. The other Advisors, thrown into a great confusion and panic, scattered and scurried about the room in what capacity they were able, each being somewhat impaired by his injuries while Hassock, quite horrified, stood rooted to the spot. Heefeeheefee, impassioned but outnumbered, was quickly cut down. The Commander, drawing again his saber, began to strike at his helmet with the flat of the blade in obvious consternation.

"An ambush, then!" cried the Commander. "A trick! Well, you'll soon learn what sad wages are earned by such efforts!" Then, turning on his heel, he beat a hasty retreat through the open door, trailing the others behind him.

"We're done for now," said one of the Advisors, a man named Huggluglug, who upon Heefeeheefee's death was next to inherit the title and responsibilities of the King's Most Trusted Advisor, when the Commander and the soldiers with him were gone. "We might as well throw ourselves from the highest tower, or drown ourselves in the moat."

"He's right," the other Advisors agreed. And, turning to consider Heefeeheefee's prostrate and lifeless form, they wept bitterly at the path on which they had been unwillingly set, and the fate to which they were seemingly irrefutably bound. "We're goners, we're done for, the jig is up, all hope is lost!"

"I suppose there's nothing more for it, then," said Hassock, slumping listlessly upon the throne. "The King's lands will be forfeit and His beautiful Castle destroyed. How can such injustice exist? It seems an affront to nature and to Heaven!" And, turning his face skyward, he issued a silent entreaty to his Maker that all subjects of the Kingdom, both present and absent, be spared such misfortune and that the advancing army, for causes obvious or otherwise, leave off its attack and return to the place from whence it had traveled, all the while and simultaneously cursing his luck that by virtue of his birth it was the departed King, and not himself, who held Divine favor and might more aptly and more compellingly bend the ear of God.

38.
The Commander, Returning...

The Commander, returning in a state of great excitement, ordered that the cannons be loaded and fired, and that the archers take their positions, and that the various and experimental devices be again employed, and that in all a full assault be levied at the soonest possible opportunity. Accordingly a great hail of arrows was sent over the Castle wall, and many peasants (who had, as the King ordered before his death, and the wish carried out by those Advisors who wished to honor his memory, been let inside the Castle walls, though the vast majority bore the unmistakable symptoms of the new pandemic) were struck and wounded, and many killed, and several others knocked to the ground and trod upon in the panic that followed. Similarly a great many of the livestock (which had been brought inside as well, both for their safety and so as to provide a food source for the populace should the battle become entrenched and otherwise untenable, and a number of which bore lesions on their extremities, and some on their bodies) were struck, and their number greatly reduced, and all present despaired that in the end insufficient food would remain to provide sustenance to the survivors. These lamentations were quickly supplanted, however, by more pressing concerns, as the experimental machines began again to launch their deadly missiles, each of which landed with sufficient force and accuracy to obliterate its target, and great holes were produced in the domed towers, and also in the Castle walls, through which the advancing army advanced, killing peasant and solider alike, until the courtyard was secured and the gate lowered, and the Commander able to ride his horse through the gates, announced by trumpets and flanked by a grand procession of fellow Officers and armored guards.

"Where is your King?" the Commander demanded. "Let Him come forth and kiss my boot, if He seeks my mercy! Otherwise the ax is swift, and apt to fall!"

"I'm right here," said Hassock, emerging from the hall in which he had sheltered throughout the bombardment. "I'm coming." And, hurrying to stand before the Commander, he bent and kissed the Commander's rather soiled boot, for which effort he received both the assembled peasantry's collective rebuke and the Commander's disdainful kick.

"Very well," said the Commander, laughing as Hassock clutched at his now bleeding mouth, "your lands and Castle, what is left of it, now belong to King Isthisthis of Isthinrod, and you may all consider yourselves subject of same." And, plucking the Crown from Hassock's head, he led his column into the inner courtyard and here dismissed them to take what pleasures and what riches they might.

At this command the occupying force fell upon the citizenry, and took what pleasures and what riches they could, and the women and the children cried, and the men were held at sword point and advised not to interfere, and fires were made and animals slaughtered and roasted, and the Royal larder raided, and many fine tapestries set ablaze, and the King's best bed irreparably defiled, and the Advisors were dressed as clowns and forced to act in the most humiliating fashion, and Hassock himself mocked unbearably, and patronized with fawning obeisance, and beaten quite savagely, through which trials he prayed for the Lord God's intervention, at which exclamations his warders laughed in the most malicious fashion, and beat him more soundly, until it was impossible to tell the lesions he'd had before the assault from the many wounds he received in the hours following.

"This is the end," cried Hassock, when the soldiers tired of him and left him alone. "All I ever wished from life for myself was that I might act as a true and a faithful servant to the King. Now the King is dead, and I suffer humiliations meant for Him. Perhaps such is a greater service than all that I have previously rendered! Yet it does seem a wage ill-befitting efforts noble and honest as mine have been. Nor does it befit a just God to abandon His humble servant here, in his darkest hour." And, mired in such dark and desperate rumination, he fell again to picking at the many sores populating his legs and arms, discovering as he did so a great number now apparent on his chest and stomach, a fact which, though frightening in its implication, arrived upon him at a moment of such despondency that its import could lower his mood no further.

39.
Upon the Western Shore of the Infinite Lake

The reconstituted ship, encountering no obstacle, made easy passage across the Infinite Lake and arrived upon the western shore with its crew all present and accounted for (save for one peasant who went missing, but who often drank to excess and in all likelihood fell over the railing in the night and so was drowned, and in any event of whose death those remaining agreed that all onboard were blameless) and the head still swinging from its mast. Making berth, the assembly swam ashore and here fell to talking amongst themselves, for drawing so near to their home it seemed (in their collective reckoning) that a dark cloud hung over the place, and that their lives there were rank and profitless, and held no joy, and might be easily forsaken.

"I feel as though there is nothing there for me anymore," said one of the remaining peasants, whose name was Hadcadfadtad. "How shall I again shelter within four walls, sleep beneath a changeless roof, when I have traveled far and seen much?"

"It is not uncommon," agreed one of the two remaining warriors, whose name was Hijjijji. "One travels abroad and sees things that he cannot find in his native land, and upon returning feels ill-fitted to his former familiar environs. It is the traveller's curse, that he must feel alienated by nature from the home he has yearned for in his far-roaming heart."

"Yes," agreed the others, "a curse if ever one existed!"

Upon this shared declaration the party agreed that it would make no further progress, for it was well understood that to move into the Great Forest would likewise be to fall under the surveillance of the King's scouts and spies, and news of their arrival would surely reach the Royal ear, and they would then be compelled (by Royal order, if not by force) to return. Camp was made, and a great fire set, and the discussion then fell to the exact nature of their shared malaise, and whether that malaise might in some way be alleviated by less dramatic means, for it did seem to all present, upon further consideration, a shameful waste to forsake so wondrous a prize over so intangible an objection.

"I just don't know what's wrong with me," said one of the remaining peasants, a man named Hufdeehufdee. "I've thought ceaselessly of my wife and children, and when the head came into our possession my heart leapt only at the thought of the life I might provide for them once I had claimed my share of the prize. Yet now that we draw nearer to home, I feel in my imaginings none of the attendant warmth and joy which should accompany such a homecoming. Instead, my heart rails against the thought of return as against the specter of imprisonment! Have I gone mad in my travels? Has the Devil cursed me with a hardened heart, so that I may never again embrace wife and son with unreserved joy?"

"If He has cursed you then He has surely cursed us all," replied the other of the two remaining warriors, whose name was Higgletyhigglety, "for my heart cries out with a similar complaint, and my mind must compel my feet to turn toward that which they should, if given leave to follow their nature, fly with unchecked passion. I fear that something dark has come upon us, that we feel such aversion."

At that moment the wind changed, and a smell descended upon the camp so rank and foul that it set all present to retching, and their eyes to watering, and their throats to burning.

"Great God!" cried Hufdeehufdee, clutching at his burning eyes. "The Devil is surely come amongst us! Run, comrades! Run and save your souls!" and with this declaration he dove into the lake and fell to thrashing about in the shallows.

There followed a scene of terrific confusion, for the peasants ran this way and that attempting to outrun their immaterial foe, while Hijjijji drew his sword and began to slash wildly and blindly at the air above his head.

"It is no Devil!" cried Higgletyhigglety, himself running into the shallows and splashing water into his eyes and mouth. "Listen to me, all of you! It is no Devil that comes upon us, only the specter of our own past violence! We have anchored farther north than the point along the shore from which we set sail, but any sailor knows how the wind can carry a smell across empty water. What we smell now is the many dead protesting from their un-revered and un-sanctified graves."

"It matters little the cause," contested Hijjijji, dropping his sword and kneeling and retching upon the sand. "Be it a natural phenomenon or demonic curse, I can stand it no longer!"

"Yes!" cried the peasants, "We will surely go mad!"

At that moment the wind lifted, and the smell dispersed as quickly as it had arrived. The congregation, reconvening around the fire, emptied water from their boots and wrung it from their clothes, and blinked away the tears still rising in their stinging eyes.

"A fouler stench I have never encountered," said Hijjijji. "Whether we return to the Castle or again set sail I care little, so long as we place some distance between us and the horror from which that wretched wind has blown."

"It is an affront to Heaven and to nature," said Higgletyhigglety. "The dead protest our ill treatment of them. Such abhorrent crimes we have enacted that the very earth yawns and refuses the dust to which, it is said, men return when they die. I fear that this passing unpleasantness is only the lightest whisper of the punishment that awaits us, in this world or the next."

"Best not to dwell on it," replied Hijjijji. "None present may grant any other absolution, or by some trick free him from the claim of these crimes. Until such a man is found, it profits us little to stand looking back at that which cannot now be altered. I say we put our thoughts to the decision at hand, and tarry no longer in doing so. Shall we turn our steps toward home, or linger a while in the broader world?"

"I still say that I cannot return," said Hufdeehufdee.

"Nor can I," agreed Hadcadfadtad.

"Nor shall we," agreed the six other peasants who had survived, and who until now had mostly kept their opinions to themselves. "Our homes lie not within the village, nor the Castle walls. Our hearts are restless and will continue on."

"In that case," said Higgletyhigglety, "you've no use for the head or the prize it will bring. I propose then that all those wishing to claim the prize should do so, and receive no argument from those to whom the head holds no use. Any wishing to continue on may claim the ship as recompense, and we will part with clear accord and kind regards."

"I hardly think that's fair," said Hufdeehufdee.

"Nor I," agreed Hadcadfadtad.

"Nor we," agreed the six peasants.

"Well then," said Hijjijji, "what do you propose?"

"Suppose we were to send an emissary to the Castle," said Hufdeehufdee, "to inform the King that Hazaiah's head has been claimed, and lies a day's ride through the Great Forest, but that the prize is to be shared among ten, some of whom do not wish to return, and so the prize must be given a monetary value equivalent to its entire value, which may then be divided into equal shares."

"An excellent suggestion," agreed Hadcadfadtad, while the six other peasants voiced their accord. "That seems the best answer, and fairest to all involved."

"And yet such seems grossly unfair to those who do return to the Castle," replied Hijjijji, "for once one equates gold to the prize's intangible aspects, namely the offered title, rank, and accommodations, then the returning parties may not claim those amenities, and something more is lost in the conversion whose absence is not felt by those who do not return. Which is to say, perhaps the parties who choose to tarry on should make some consolation to those returning, to lessen the sting of this lessened reward."

"Balderdash!" replied the peasants, in outrage. "Poppycock!"

"I think it only fair," agreed Higgletyhigglety.

"I, too," agreed Hijjijji.

Just as the argument began to grow heated the wind shifted, and the nauseating smell again settled upon the camp, and sent the inhabitants scurrying for the shallows. Here they remained for some minutes, gagging and gasping, and also vomiting up what dinner they'd had, and rubbing their eyes and plugging up their noses. There was as well a general outcry, and many declarations that nothing further would be tolerated, and that a decision had to be made, so that when the noxious cloud lifted all trudged back to the fire with singular intent and sorely tested patience, not to mention a lack of good humor, and sat wringing water from their clothing and emptying it from their boots in silence, for it was apparent that the first to speak would be loudly and roundly rebuked for his effort.

"All I'm going to say," offered Hijjijji, after several silent minutes had passed, "is that some concession should be made. How much is another matter entirely, and certainly open to discussion."

"A pact!" cried the peasants, in sudden and violent eruption. "We had an accord, an agreement, a contract! No man would profit more than any other! The prize would be shared equally by all!"

"But that is precisely what I'm saying," protested Hijjijji, straining to be heard over the uproar. "By leaving with an equal share of gold those who do not return profit more than those who remain and must return to their old environs, having been denied their claim to more Regal accommodations by virtue of the conversion."

This well-reasoned and patiently-delivered argument made no progress against the peasants' cries, and Hijjijji soon left off all attempts and fell silent. The peasants, however, grew more vocal in this silence, and began to shout amongst themselves and at the warriors all of their most heartfelt objections and accusations, and set to calling the warriors unpleasant names, and saying that such had been the plan all along, that the warriors had always intended to take the lion's share of the prize, once it was claimed, and that they (the peasants) would not stand for it. These insults, however, soon proved fatal, for Higgletyhigglety (who had been regarding the peasants' diatribe with lessening humor) drew his sword and with a powerful thrust slew Hufdeehufdee, who was the most vocal and the most pernicious of the peasants. At this the assembly fell into great confusion, with the peasants attacking the warriors, and Hijjijji was forced to draw his sword and defend himself, and in so doing struck down four of the remaining seven, while Higgletyhigglety slew three, so that the count was evenly distributed among them, and in the scuffle the head was knocked into the fire and set ablaze, and badly charred, before Higgletyhigglety, dispatching with the last peasant, drew it from the fire on his sword point and doused it in the lake, where it hissed and bubbled the surface, and from which it emerged quite unrecognizable, being in many places only a blackened skull.

"Well then," said Higgletyhigglety, breathing quite heavily after such violent exertion. "I suppose then the argument is settled, for better or for worse. Shall we put this place to our heels, and lessen the trek that lies before us?"

"I bet my soul that I want nothing further from my life," replied Hijjijji, "than that I put my back to this place and never return so long as I live."

Collecting what few necessities remained (and placing the head in a new sack, the old one having been destroyed in the fire) the two set off into the Great Forest, each dispelling the insistent unsettling thoughts that haunted and troubled him with visions of the Castle and the prize that waited there.

40.

In the Morning, They Were Startled To Discover...

In the morning, members of the occupying force were startled to discover innumerable red and black sores covering their wrists and ankles. They called upon the Doctor, who advised a series of bleedings which left many of them listless and pale, and quite unequipped for the rather sizable task of putting the Castle into some semblance of cleanliness and order. This troubled the Commander not in the least, for it seemed a far better thing for the conquered peoples to perform such unpleasant and difficult tasks. He called upon the Squadron Leader, and instructed him to rouse what nobles and peasants he could find and put them to work. The Squadron Leader returned some time later, however, and informed the Commander that few could be found who were fit enough to work, and that many had expired in the night in what seemed to be a ghastly and violent way, for the corpses were covered with numerous gaping sores, many of which seemed to have burst and bled, by which course these afflicted had died. All of this the Squadron Leader spoke while scratching his own sores, and the Commander regarded while picking at those present on his own ankles and wrists, and the Doctor was summoned and asked what he thought it meant, to which he could give no reply, though he was interrupted several times by the Deacon who, forcing his way into the room, shouted that the Devil was surely in it, and that they should leave this place at once, to which the Commander laughed and explained that one did not simply abandon the lands one went through such efforts to conquer and claim.

Meanwhile, outside, members of the invading army (being overwhelmed in their fevered state by a powerful thirst, and having poisoned all of the wells during their invasion) took to drinking directly from the moat, a course which (owing to the many bodies and limbs which lay bloated and rotting on the moat's muddy bottom) exacerbated, accelerated, and internalized the disease's progress, and these soldiers soon died in agony, complaining of powerful stomach pains, and coughing and vomiting blood, which upon posthumous examination appeared to relate to large sores which had formed along the inside of their throats and digestive tracts, at the discovery of which the Doctor forbade everyone from drinking from the moat, a directive which came too late for many, some of whom collapsed in fear (having witnessed first-hand the horrific fate that now awaited them) and waited for death to come, and some of whom went to church and prayed vehemently for salvation, and some of whom threw themselves from the tallest tower, so that in all several dozen souls lost their lives by the end of the first day, with several dozen others barely clinging to life, and a great wailing and lamenting was heard, and also a great outcry against the King and the Commander, who had brought them to this fate, during which the Commander locked himself in the Royal bedchamber, and picked and scratched at his own worsening sores, and struck his helmet with the flat of his saber, and wondered what he should do.

41.
Hijjijji and Higgletyhigglety

While the soldiers mourned and bemoaned their plight, and while the Commander struck at his helmet with the flat of his saber, and while the Doctor performed one bloodletting after another, and the surviving peasants tended indifferently to the wounds they had received in the battle, and also picked at the sores growing now on their torsos, and some on their necks and faces, and while the smell of the new dead mingled with the smell of the old dead, and permeated every hall and chamber so that even the Commander, high up in the King's bedchamber, was not spared, Hijjijji and Higgletyhigglety sat beside their fire and considered the head, which they had set on a stump between them.

"It might be anyone," said Hijjijji. "There's hardly enough flesh left on it to know that it was a man. Suppose the King doesn't believe us, and we're given nothing for our trouble? You know as well as I do what moods the King is prone to!"

"Quiet yourself," replied Higgletyhigglety. "Such thoughts profit us nothing, in our present circumstances, and to give them voice only tempts the Devil to make them so. Hazaiah is dead, and news of his demise has surely reached the King's ear. Himself being so prepared, He will doubtless believe that this charred skull belonged to the man himself, for He has little reason to doubt. There is no other, I might remind you, to lay claim to the prize, and so our voice, ringing out in solitude, will likewise ring with the knell of truth. Further, ask yourself why the King called for Hazaiah's head. Was it the head that He yearned for, or rather proof of the vassal's demise? Surely the latter, and if news has reached Him of same then He has every reason to rejoice and no reason to call us liar."

"Your reasoning reassures me," replied Hijjijji. "Truly, we have little to fear."

At that moment a sound in the forest, originating from beyond the reach of the fire's light, made both men stand and draw their weapons. Demanding of the source its nature and intentions, the warriors received in reply only a grating whisper, as of a throat unaccustomed to speech, as though an animal was trying to respond. Taking a burning log from the fire Hijjijji ventured into the forest and there discovered a shrunken and aged and unkept man who, though he wore no clothes, was saved from immodesty by his beard, which had grown to such a length that he was able to wrap it about his middle in the fashion of a loincloth. This man retreated and cowered from the flame and the brandished blade, but was soon placated (when the warriors saw that there was nothing to fear) by kind words and the sheathing of swords, and was encouraged to join the warriors by their fire, and give some account of himself and his strange circumstances, which after some further prompting he did. He had no sooner begun his tale, however, than Higgletyhigglety let out a great cry and fell off his log.

"Great God!" he shouted, regaining his seat. "Do my eyes deceive me? Have my many weeks of wandering compelled me into madness? For it is not some humble hermit which I see seated before me but the King's father Himself, in the flesh, the Royal bearing and visage like unto no other!"

"Heavens above!" shouted Hijjijji, moving somewhat closer to the man to study his features. "The Roman nose, the Noble lips, the brow creased by the Crown which sat upon it! It is the King the King's father, and no other, or I am not myself!"

"Yes," answered the man, in a voice little more than a whisper. "I am that unfortunate soul, who sired one so wretched! But calm yourselves and sit, and I will relate to you the sad progress of my years, which have led me to such miserable habits as you see, that I sit before you now naked and filthy, a mere shadow of myself in my former glory!"

"Tell, Good King!" replied the warriors, seating themselves and staring in unblinking wonder. "Tell us all, and do not pause until your tongue has rendered forth its final word!"

"I will tell," said the old man.

42.
The King the King's Father's Story

"If I am to tell," began the King the King's father, "then I must impart to you in no unclear terms the nature of the man who bears my Crown, and in so doing must render forth a secret which, if widely put out, would surely be the author of much calamity. My wife the Blessed Queen, being in the full bloom of her fertility, did conceive a child which was to be heir to all my lands and wealth and power. This child, unborn, did we dote upon with all the affections of expectant parents, and prepared for him all manner of luxury which our Royal purse could supply. Yet these generous offerings made no peace between us, for the child was born with such violence, such calamity and opposition that the Doctor could broker no appeasement. Likewise he was compelled to cut child from mother's womb, which efforts bore no fruit, for the child died upon the instant, being of lesser mettle than his father, and my Queen did pass from life, they say, as much from a broken heart as from the Doctor's knife.

"I was, at that time, in my own full bloom of vitality and virility, and - it is no secret - often let my gaze wander o'er servant girl and chambermaid alike. As it happened, of these there was one in whom my seed took root and grew, in very near to the same hour as that seed which, grown and plucked from the tree, destroyed both self and life-giving tree in one terrible instant. So it was this other child, birthed with ease and set wailing upon the earth, that was placed in my arms: this child - born not of Queen but of servant girl - that was introduced to my loyal and expectant subjects as my son. But truth cloaked in artifice loses claim to truth! For it was given out as well that this son was born of the Blessed Queen, for whom my heart still wept, and that He (being of full and Noble blood) should likewise follow after me when my days achieved their end.

"This arrangement, reached between the child's chambermaid mother and my Most Trusted Advisor (while I, quite prostrated by grief, refused all discourse), became the very thorn which, lodged in my side, continued to prick and sting me all my days upon the throne. For mother would only give over child if she might tend to it, become its nanny, play at mother in the Queen's absence: in short, remain the mother which she was, receiving all the due and luxury attendant to the Son of a King, and moreover in this fashion retain her poisonous influence, for I was soon to learn that in my lustful ways I had blindly laid atop a viper whose jaws concealed such steely and cunning fangs as would pluck the Crown from atop my still-pulsating brain!

"The child grew, and in growing presented such a perfect and artful mask of restraint and piety and fealty that I gladly clutched him to my breast and called him Son and Prince and Heir. I attempted in my way to teach him all that I had learned in my years seated betwixt throne and Crown, told him of the importance of moderation, of considered council, of the need to keep a dispassionate manner so as not to be drawn into a quarrel unnecessarily. All I told him and all he received, and nodded his head, and batted his lashes, and kissed my cheek with such poison-concealing artifice as one finds nowhere else in nature, for at night his mother told him other things, instructed him in such wiles as her gender had engendered her and which she herself had cultivated, and in this fashion plotted and maneuvered, so that his dreams were treasonous and unwholesome.

"So it was that in the winter of the child's fourteenth year I rode into the lands north of the Kingdom, near unto our border with Geefeenee. The child and its mother were by my side, and my guards had fallen some distance behind. So it happened that, far from any aid, the child's mother notched arrow to bowstring and felled me. This deed done she let out a great cry and turned her mount, riding back in the direction from which we'd come, with the child hard at her heels. I lay dazed (I had struck my head in falling, and for some time could not compel my limbs to move), contenting myself with the notion that soon the guards would come to recover my body and, finding me yet living, would return me to my kingdom and my throne, from where I might do just service to the treasonous vixen. Yet no guard came, and by nightfall I found that my movement and dexterity had been restored. Likewise I roused myself and, dislodging the arrow from where it had struck me (the wound was trifling, and would never have achieved its end but that the blow I received in falling addled my brains) I took shelter for the night, for my horse had run off, and I could not proceed far on foot, for the darkness was so complete and oppressive that I might have o'er stepped the cliff's edge with no notion of impending disaster."

"This I recall most clearly," put in Hijjijji. "It was widely put out that you had been slain by soldiers from

Geefeenee, and that your body could not be recovered for fear that more lives would be lost in the effort."

"It is then as I later concluded," replied the King the King's Father, nodding his head. "I wonder only how long she had been planning to spring such a trap on me, all while I clutched our child ever-closer to me, all while she shared my bed!"

"It is truly a sad tale," agreed Higgletyhigglety. "But please continue, Good King, and tell how you came to such low and strange circumstances as those in which we now find you."

"But I am certain that you already know the bulk of the matter, or could guess it," replied the King the King's father. "This manufactured enmity with Geefeenee was compelled toward violent quarrel, and this done with such haste that my two days' journey homeward did not o'erstep the soldiers' dispatch. Likewise I arrived to find my Castle gate barred and my guards suspicious of my story and my claims. I was brought before my son (on whose head the Crown now sat, and in whose ear his mother yet poured her venom) and here decried (my heart broke to hear it, and I cursed my former lechery!) as an impostor, a spy sent from Geefeenee, an impious knave who would mock a son's pain with so gross a display. This I heard and was amazed, and at this his mother smiled, and the guards fell upon me and dragged me to the dungeon far below, where I was kept for many days, one leading into the next until I could no longer perceive their sum, until the unwarranted quarrel came home to roost, and Geefeenee soldiers stormed the Castle, and in the confusion I managed my escape.

"I fled into the Great Forest, and for a time kept hope that I would one day and by some miracle be restored to all that I had lost, and it to me. With such dreams I kept my sanity for as long as any man might, being forced to endure such injustice and sorrow, before despair o'ercame my good senses and I collapsed into a prolonged madness in which I forgot even what it was to be a man, forgot even the use of God's blessed gifts of speech and reason. In this madness I lived and might well have lived out my days, but that I recently encountered a traveler to whom I offered some aid. For my efforts I was soundly and most unjustly beaten, nearly unto death, and it was only when I emerged from the resultant stupor (in which I lay for I don't know how long) that I found myself, by some phenomenon of my abused and throbbing brain, restored to my former mind, with all attendant skill and constitution and emotion returned to me."

"God be praised!" intoned the warriors.

"Yes," agreed the King the King's father, "His good works are like the blessed sunshine after the storm! But look upon me, gentle Sirs, and you will perceive that such blessings wax poor when housed in so shameful a vessel! What would I do, in such a state? Approach the Castle gates with professions of my sanity? Broach idle wanderers with pleasant greetings? No! Since my restoration have I been lurking in my shame in the shadows, far from any traveler, yearning for one shred of that former animal immodesty that for so long held seated command in my much-altered brain, that would approach man or beast with little regard for accustomed social graces! I beg of you, good Sirs, if I may lean heavier upon your mercy and your hospitality, bestow upon me some disused clothing so that I might clothe my nakedness and walk as a man does once again, before my days have all passed from me!"

"Certainly!" cried HIjjijji.

"At once!" agreed Higgletyhigglety, and in a moment the two had retrieved from their rucksacks enough clothing to cover the old man.

"May God's eternal blessings shine upon you," said the King the King's father, weeping tears of gratitude. "In my darkest hour I felt certain that I would never again feel the warm breath of human kindness. It is like unto a sunburst in my very soul to know that I was wrong!"

"It is a trifling thing, and one gladly done for our better," replied Higgletyhigglety. "But now that we have heard your story we must retire, for we have business with the King your son in the morning, and I fear we will need our strength to argue for our claim."

"If you go to see my son, then let me steel you," replied the King the King's father. "Trust not the words of his lips, for they trumpet always with another and a lower melody which the King alone hears and which holds the truth of the matter. Trust neither the word of his mother, if she is yet living, for she is the more cunning of the two, and her poison twice as deadly. Trust neither any promise given, nor any reward that seems too grand, for it was a favorite game of his as a child (and how I curse and have cursed mine own eyes that I did not regard the warning in it, or acknowledge the cruel nature it revealed!) to draw in some peasant child and lavish upon him all the trappings of Royalty, only to take them away again and cast the child out of doors, delighting in the poor child's screams and entreaties. A cruel disposition owns my son, an icy patina that father's love could never thaw nor chip its way through. I charge you: be on your guard, and trust not his word, but collect what favor your may in gold that you may cart away, and accept not the promise of favors for which you must remain and attend upon him, for they will be so hard in coming that it would be better to have never courted them at all."

"None know son better than father!" replied the warriors. "We would be fools indeed to disregard such wise advice so generously given."

"As for myself," continued the old man, "I fear that time has worn away like the ever-flowing river upon the rock bed the steadfast and, I once thought, irreducible character of my anger. For many a wasted year I warmed my chilled features with thoughts of the retribution I might enact upon him that bore my Crown. Yet I find now that the fire that once so enlivened me has all but embered, and in searching I discover there no spark with which to light a greater fire, nor fuel to feed it, nor will to resurrect it. In short I am an old man, and tire now bearing as I do the bulk of these years upon my head. Thus I wish you God's favor, and commend you to your fortune, and beg of you your leave." Here he rose and, giving no backward glance, moved once again into the shadows and was lost from sight.

"Poor man!" said Higgletyhigglety, when he'd gone. "One imagines the King to live a blessed and a carefree life, couched as He is in unending luxury. Perhaps it is more blessed indeed, as Christ our Lord instructed his Disciples, to be poor and meek, and to seek one's reward in Heaven and not upon the earth."

"Truly, it is something to consider," replied HIjjijji. "But come: we have a day before us, and one in which I fear lay trials and snares of which we are yet ignorant and whose nature we, being but men, and having only a vision of present and past but none of future, cannot guess. Still, were I like unto the wizard, whose more-than-mortal eye peers further than other men's eyes, I might more regard the ache now troubling my guts, and read there some premonition of disaster. Let us go to our rest, and in being rested perhaps keep ourselves from that other rest which, I fear, may meet us in the course of this errand."

"Yes," agreed Higgletyhigglety, "I too sense some terrible and impending calamity. Yet we have not traveled so far and endured so much to abandon our quest in the final hour. Let us regard well what the King the King's father has said, and keep a watchful eye, and by being prepared skirt the pitfalls which may litter our path. But now: to bed."

"Yes, to bed," agreed Hijjijji. "Thus will we pass the night, and see what the morning brings." Then, taking the head from the stump and clutching it tightly to his breast, he lay down beside the fire and fell asleep.

43.
That Night...

That night several dozen peasants died in agony, bleeding from their lesions, and their screams filled the courtyard, and rose unchecked, and entered the open air-congress, and traversed the threshold to the stately Royal bedchamber, disturbing as they did the Commander, whose own lesions had grown considerably, and proceeded further to echo amongst the gilded and badly-damaged domes topping the Castle's few remaining towers, before they rose, unhindered, into the dark and still and insensate heavens.

"This cannot long endure," muttered the Commander, laying awake in the King's bed, dabbing at the blood oozing from his sores with the edge of the King's best linen. "There'll be no one left, before long. This is an unseemly business we've gotten ourselves into. I'm all for conquest! But this seems to me to be something else altogether, and in truth I wish that the Noble Lord King Isthisthis had never sent me!" And here, forgetting himself in his terror, he began to sob and tear at his hair, and also to curse his King and the whole of the land of Isthinrod, throwing himself into such fits of passion that his chest began to heave, and the many lesions there to stretch and burst, and much of his own blood was spilled and the King's best linens were irreparably stained. "Oh unhappy day that I was ever born!" he cried, and fell to making pleas to God, and entreating His mercy, and offering various compromises should his life be spared.

Far below the King's bedchamber the peasants and the soldiers milled aimlessly about the courtyard, intermingling indiscriminately. Everyone was looking for the Doctor, but the Doctor was nowhere to be found. In the dungeon beneath their feet Hassock clutched the King's robe's more tightly about his shoulders, for he felt a chill which it seemed no heat could lessen. He called to the guard to bring the brazier closer, but the guard gave no reply, and when he dragged himself to the bars (opening as he did many small wounds amongst the blisters on his legs) he could not see the guard anywhere. His annoyance and frustration at this fact were lessened considerably by the profound exhaustion this meager effort had produced. He lay against the bars, hoping that the guard would return soon. Some time later the sun crested the horizon, and spilled in through the small barred window in Hassock's cell, and roused Hassock from shallow sleep. Pressing his face to the bars he called out to the other prisoners, inquiring after their health, and whether anyone knew the location of the guard. To these efforts he received no reply. He pulled himself to his feet and made several more attempts, each with the same result. Seating himself again upon the floor he was surprised to discover a great quantity of blood issuing from beneath the robe, from the lesions that populated his chest and stomach. He was surprised because, unlike all occasions previous, these fresh wounds gave him no pain.

Outside the Castle wall various animals, some from the village and some from the forest beyond, that during the night had come to drink from the moat, now became bloated and died, with great streams of blood issuing from their mouths.   This the peasants and soldiers observed with wonder, for such a strange and miraculous sight certainly seemed a sign, though of what no one present was of adequate authority in matters scientific or religious to posit or postulate.

44.

Hazaiah's Head

The great drawbridge lay across the moat, the portcullis had been drawn away, no guard paced the battlements; the soldiers, lethargic with disease, lay wherever they had been standing when fatigue overcame them. Some had arrived at the blight's final stage, and so sprawled in pools of their own blood and gore, while others had simply frozen to death in the night's chill, their disease-exhausted bodies having no will left to warm them. Still others lingered on the edge of life, and so could offer some guidance to those who, arriving in ignorance, now wished to know the story of the Castle's ruin. None could offer any information, however, as to the fate of the King, or where He might now be found. The travelers were therefore sent instead to the King's bedchamber and told to inquire of the Commander, who it was said most certainly knew the answer to their question.

"The King," moaned the Commander, writhing upon the bed and opening as he did many wounds along his back and torso. "Heaven deliver me! I cannot stand it any longer! The King has been - Oh God, it's nearly unbearable! - sent to the dungeon, as is befitting any conquered Ruler. Lord have mercy!"

"The dungeon," said Higgletyhigglety, shaking his head in wonder.

"Truly there has been some horror here which we, busy lamenting our own misfortunes, failed to imagine," replied Hijjijji.

"Oh merciful Heavenly Father!" cried the Commander.

"Come, let us see to Him who was once our better," said Higgletyhigglety, "and show Him that His charge has been faithfully carried out, for though it seems now certain that there's no reward in it, I am anxious to put my heels to this place, and will not have done so until that cursed thing is with He who sought it."

"Yes," agreed Hijjijji, "and let's be rid of it quickly, too, for it has in truth been naught but the father of tragedy and disaster."

Leaving the still-whimpering Commander they exited the bedchamber and descended to the dungeon. Encountering no guard they entered and there found Hassock in his cell, wrapped in the King's robes, his face so altered by blisters and fatigue that even if they had known the King well they might not have known that it was not he who lay before them.

"Your Majesty," said Higgletyhigglety, reaching through the bars and touching Hassock lightly on the arm to rouse him, at which the prisoner let out a cry and clutched at the place, at which motion he let out several more cries, for the blisters along his back and chest had been torn by his sudden movement.

"What woeful misfortune is this!" lamented Hijjijji, and here he began to weep, for it broke his heart to see his beloved King so poorly used. "Great God, where is your favor now? What has become of Your infinite mercy?" And he fell to cursing God and Heaven and all of the clerics he had ever known.

"Silence yourself," replied Higgletyhigglety, "for but observe His face and you will see that your blasphemies greatly offend our King!" Then, kneeling before the bars, he drew the head from its sack and held it up for the prisoner to see. "Your Majesty," he said, "Your bidding is done, Your faithful servants return with that which Your Majesty, with unblemished lips, did once beseech us to retrieve. Here I offer it to Your Majesty for, though Your Majesty may no more reward make, I take as sufficient recompense the knowledge that I did serve my King well, and gave to Him that which no other might."

"Yes," agreed Hijjijji, leaving off his cursing of Heaven. "And I, too."

Hassock, reaching through the bars, took the offered skull and considered it for some time, more out of necessity than interest, for every movement caused him great pain, and he was forced to move very slowly, and to turn the skull about in small and halting increments. Moreover he seemed, by his blank and changeless expression, to be unable to make any reckoning of the object in his hands, and the warriors awaited his reply nervously, more out of habit than reason, for the King's word still held (for them) its accustomed weight and authority, and (despite the impotence of his situation) it seemed impossible that his disappointment would not result in some great misfortune being visited upon them. Finally his inspection was complete, and the whole of the boney and badly-damaged trophy had been considered, from the jaws (which had offered the warriors hospitality) to the hole in the crested top (through which Hazaiah's lifeblood had finally and fatally flowed) and Hassock, steeling himself against the pain which was certain to accompany the effort, opened his mouth to speak.

"I've no way of knowing if this is Hazaiah's," he said. "There isn't enough flesh left upon it to tell this from any other. This skull could belong to anyone."

"But Your Majesty," protested Hijjijji, "You have our word that it is his and no other!"

"Yes," agreed Higgletyhigglety, "our word!"

This judgement, however, seemed to have wholly exhausted the reclining potentate, for he gave only a rattling cough in reply. The warriors, rising from where they had knelt amongst the straw and filth, stood and considered their King, who now seemed to be laying very still, and also bleeding a great deal, so much so that the blood soaked through the heavy and ornate robe he wore. Bowing one final time they exited the dungeon, and stepping out into the warm sunshine they felt as though a tremendous burden had been taken from them, as though a shroud had been lifted from the world. Their anger and indignation (that their weeks of effort and travail had produced no reward) remained behind them in the dungeon's shadows, and in the open courtyard they could only feel how pleasant and how blessed it was to be living when so many were dead, and how wonderful it was to feel breath in one's lungs and the earth beneath one's feet. Treading their way between the corpses they left the courtyard, and entered the village, and there, after some searching, discovered enough food to make a simple but bountiful meal, and a hut which had not been wholly destroyed, so that that night they slept beneath a roof for the first time in many weeks, and awoke in the morning well-rested and satisfied, and it was only upon rising that each discovered a number of small red-and-black blisters covering his wrists and ankles.

"This is your fault!" cried Hijjijji, drawing his dagger. "I told you that my gut said something like this would happen if we continued on to the Castle, but you didn't listen!"

"If you will recall," replied Higgletyhigglety, also drawing his dagger, "I also professed a deep-seated trepidation about our errand, and it was decided amongst us that we would see the endeavor through to the end."

"I don't care!" cried Hijjijji, who was now crying quite uncontrollably. "It's your fault all the same! Now I've got what killed them all, and you've done it to me! My death is upon you!"

"I have it as well!" shouted Higgletyhigglety in reply, lifting his trouser cuff to show the blisters encircling his ankle. "Your plight is my own! If your death is upon me then likewise mine falls upon you!"

"No!" wailed Hijjijji, who now seemed divested of all vitality, and fell to his knees. "God would not have allowed me to survive so much, only to let me die in this violent and horrible fashion!" and here his sobs wholly overwhelmed his voice, and he could make no words but instead uttered a series of inarticulate shouts and heaving sighs, so profound was his despair.

"Quiet yourself," shouted Higgletyhigglety, "for the love of all things Holy! I'll go mad if you do not leave off this wailing at once!"

Hijjijji, however, whether unsympathetic or deaf to his companion's pleas, let out in reply a prolonged and thunderous howl which, being of such extraordinary length and volume, seemed to emanate not from Hijjijji's lungs but rather from some supernatural force which, lodged in the warrior's throat, seemed capable of enduring forever, until Higgletyhigglety's mind was broken by the sheer relentless force of its cry. Likewise Higgletyhigglety fell upon his companion, and stabbed him a dozen times in the chest, as though by striking there he might murder the demon that so tormented him.

"You've killed me!" gasped Hijjijji, attempting unsuccessfully to draw breath into his perforated lungs. "Now my death comes doubly upon you!" And here he expired, bleeding out his life into the indifferent dirt.

"I told you," replied Higgletyhigglety, frantic tears welling in his eyes. "I begged you to stop! What was I supposed to do? I couldn't stand it any longer! What should I have done?" And here, in sudden revulsion and horror, he fled the village and ran weeping into the fields where, disconsolate and heartbroken, he passed four days and nights until, exhausted by hunger and cold, and tormented by guilt and ravaged by blisters, his final breath passed from his lungs and joined with the wind, where it was carried along for some time, until it lost all character of its former host, and became again the indifferent air.

45.

Master and Page

By this time Herarityrarity and Hypup, Master and Page, had traveled some distance from the Castle, and so had no inkling of the disaster that had there occurred. Pausing in the snow high atop the Hridish Pass (Herarityrarity was sweating beneath the great many clothes that he wore, while Hypup shivered in his light frock and looked longingly at his hat, which now sat atop his Master's head) Hypup commented in passing that surely someone had by now claimed the wondrous prize that the King had offered, and was certainly enjoying all of the finery that the Castle had to offer. To this comment, however, Herarityrarity let out a great bellow of hearty laughter, and fell to slapping at his sides and, eventually, to rolling around in the snow in an extravagant display of irrepressible mirth.

"I don't know what's so funny about what I said," said Hypup, shivering all the more for his hurt feelings, and still eyeing the hat which, now fallen from its bearer's head, was being rolled over and upon by the jovial Master.

"Oh, ho ho!" cried Herarityrarity, unable to contain himself. "Heehee, haha! You don't - Lord have mercy! - you don't understand! You don't know! Oh ho he ha! It's such a marvelous joke, and you can't know it!"

"Well if you simply explained it to me," replied the Page, growing bold enough in his indignation to allow an edge to enter his voice, "then perhaps I would understand. I don't think it's very nice to mock someone for their ignorance, when they've had no chance to learn that which they are being mocked for not knowing!" And here, growing even bolder, he snatched the hat from the snow and planted it firmly upon his head.

"Oh my, oh my!" said Herarityrarity, sitting up and wiping tears from his eyes, seemingly indifferent to the lost hat. "You are right of course: it is not very sporting to mock you for what you do not - and indeed, could not! - know. Were I not sworn to secrecy I might illuminate your young mind, and we might share this laugh together." And here, rising to his feet, he quickly and deftly plucked the cap from Hypup's head and placed it squarely on his own. "Now," he said, turning once again to the path, "we've a great distance to travel before nightfall and I am indeed anxious to be off, for of all things, to be stranded atop the Hridish in the dark is to invite disaster."

"But why can't you tell me what you were laughing about?" asked the Page, when they were again on their way. "You must know that, as I am your Page, and you are my Master, I am sworn to keep any secret that you might impart to me. Further I might add, although to do so seems the height of precocity, that we have encountered no one for nearly a fortnight, and that when we are again among men we will be in a foreign land, and far from any ear which would care to hear or hand which might wish to act." And with entreaties such as these he hounded his Master for the better part of three hours, during which time they achieved the crest of the Hridish Pass and began to descend the opposite side, and during which time also the sun began to set, and the shadows to grow long, and Herarityrarity to tread close to the threshold of distraction, hastened there by his Page's ceaseless pleas.

"Enough!" cried Herarityrarity, when camp had been set and a fire built, during which tasks also Hypup's petitions had failed to cease. "You have broken my resolve; I surrender! Give me but a moment's peace, a moment's silence, and I swear that I will then impart to you in full the exact and true cause of my prior merriment, whose enactment I now regret, and give to you that knowledge I previously withheld!"

"Goody!" cried Hypup, clapping his hands, and here fell silent for the first time in three hours, and sat expectantly staring at his Master, and grinning broadly, for he could hardly contain his excitement.

"It was widely put out," began Herarityrarity, "that Hazaiah, sovereign of the Kingdom's easternmost region, bore a secret enmity towards our Good King, wished Him ill, and pursuant to this sentiment gave only a pittance of a tithe in annual tax, and also orchestrated several attacks on the Castle and village, the most notable of which occurred on the twelfth of September last, the fifth of June most recent, and the eighteenth of August two years gone. Accordingly and predictably our King, being thus provoked and enraged, called for Hazaiah's head, and offered so generous a reward that no reasonable and able-bodied man would forgo an attempt. Likewise the homeland, being divested of nearly all who might, in a time of dire need, defend it, lay open and exposed to any enemy who might lay siege to it. Sometimes circumstances conspire toward ruin! Other times, however, circumstances must be nudged in the direction of most unfavorable and disastrous outcomes and, in the case of one so wanton and impiously powerful, must indeed be shoved, else no progress might be enacted against the bulwark of Monarchy. Have you ever heard, by chance, of The Guild of Loyal Subversion?"

"By that name do you mean," replied Hypup, "that band of disloyal and duplicitous traitors who plot against the Crown, the organization so secret that its name exists only in gossip and rumor, whose members have sworn a blood oath to bring down the King and rejoin His lands with the kingdoms of Isthinrod to the east and Geefeenee to the north, from which they were carved by the King's father's father, and in so doing reunite the vast Kingdom of Jifjofjif, which once encompassed the whole of the region, and return to power the deposed and exiled heir to Jifjofjif's throne, whose identity none but its members have learned?"

"The very same," replied Herarityrarity.

"I have heard of them," answered Hypup, "as every child has, whose interests trend toward the secret and the macabre. But what of it? Its existence has never been proven, and most dismiss the name with a laugh and a sneer at anyone foolish enough to believe in stories of secret societies, hidden plots, and unholy rituals."

"Our rituals are not unholy!" bellowed Herarityrarity, rising to his feet. "Rather, it is all genuflection and respect shown to the by now dethroned King which might be more rightly called blasphemous, for only the true King of Jifjofjif holds God's blessing and mandate, and all others who ordain to call themselves His earthly Proxy speak false and tempt damnation!" And here, greatly impassioned by his own speech, he began to march in a circle around the fire as he spoke, gesturing wildly in the air, which performance Hypup found most disturbing, and from which after a time he had to look away, for the motion of his Master's arms and the constant circling was making him rather nauseas. "For three generations we waited," cried Herarityrarity, "father passing on to son the true history of his homeland, imparting to him love for the True King and His Holy mandate. For three generations we have plotted and planned, biding our time until a moment arose in which the three factions of The Guild might impress upon our un-revered Kings such circumstances as would enact a chain of events leading to their collective undoing. And such have we finally achieved!" And here he let forth a great howl of laughter so unlike his previous bout of merriment, so characterized by malice, that it seemed to Hypup that, had he not borne witness to both incidents, and instead heard both sets of laughter without seeing their author, he might never have believed them to have sprung from the same man.

"Great Heaven," he said to himself, "in my haste to be of service I've squired myself out to a madman! So do I understand correctly," asked Hypup, speaking up so that he might be heard over Herarityrarity's laughter, "that it was The Guild behind the call for Hazaiah's head?"

"The Guild, and none other!" shouted Herarityrarity, in triumph. "And a masterful trick it was, for Hazaiah was indeed the most harmless and inoffensive of men, and certainly undeserving of such harsh treatment! Unfortunately for him, his lands lay far enough from the Castle, and beyond so treacherous a stretch of terrain, that any commerce between his subjects and those living in the vicinity of the Castle was highly unlikely. Thus could he be slandered and libeled, and blamed for certain plots of which he was wholly ignorant but for which, he and his subjects being absent and thus silent in his defense, he could be widely and erroneously blamed, so much so that even the King would believe the lie. As for the lacking tithe, it was a simple thing to stake out the paths through the Great Forest when tax time came, and rob the poor Porter blind, and send one of our own instead, and deliver an insulting pittance. Thus may a good man's name be ruined by villainy, and himself put into the service of a cause of which he is unaware!"

"My God!" cried Hypup. "So, if I am to understand you correctly, you are telling me that it was The Guild responsible for the attacks on the Castle and village, in which a great many lives were lost and innumerable injuries received?"

"The Guild, and none other!" repeated Herarityrarity. "We've worked our plan with devious cunning, and now go to our reward!" And here he set to executing a stomping dance around the fire in celebration of his and his comrades' success and cleverness.

"But so many have died," replied Hypup. "My own dear parents, through no fault of their own, were ensnared in the chaotic events that followed the King's decree and have been lost to me, and I fear have certainly perished. You and your compatriots have toppled forth a boulder from the mountainside, whose destructive path and final mark you could not and cannot predict. What disasters you have wrought!" And here he fell to weeping at the tragic and arbitrary circumstances which had fathered in their headlong progress all of his tribulation and woe.

"There, there," replied Herarityrarity, stepping closer and placing a comforting hand on Hypup's shoulder. "We've all made sacrifices. But what's done is done and can't be undone: I urge you instead to think of the glorious future! The True King will be restored to His throne, and The Guild will be heralded as the authors of His return, and we will all be rewarded with riches beyond comprehension. Even you, as my Page, will live ensconced in every conceivable luxury, and will never want for anything ever again."

"That does sound nice," agreed the Page, drying his eyes, and pulling his shirt more tightly across his shoulders, for the fire had begun to die and the night wind was cold. "If I may be so bold as to ask," he said, emboldened by his Master's gentle manner, "and as you are closer, and the effort a small one, would you mind setting another branch on the fire, for it is truly very cold, and my garments, I fear, are insufficient to stand against the climes."

"We've no more wood," replied his Master, looking about. "I suppose you'll have to go and gather some. I charge you to be quiet about it when you do, however, for I'm rather tired from our long climb, and will likely be asleep before long." And here, crawling into the dry space beneath a nearby tree, he pulled the Page's scarf and cape up over his head and was soon snoring.

It took several minutes for the Page to coax enough heat from the embers to thaw his numbed feet. When that was done he rose and set about his task, moving gingerly, for his toes ached and protested greatly with each step. The woods were dark, and dry wood hard to come by, and soon the Page began to despair in his search. With luck, however, and after some time, he discovered a dead tree that had toppled, whose underside branches had been protected from the snow. These he broke off and gathered, careful to make as little sound as he could, thoughtful always of his Master's request. Returning to the camp, however, he found that the fire had gone out, and no ember remained from which further flame could be roused. After some private debate (during which his feet again went numb) he crawled in beside his Master beneath the tree, and attempted to find some comfortable position in what space remained. No sooner had he entered, however, than he was pushed and kicked by his Master who, though half asleep, nevertheless objected greatly to the Page's presence. These kicks and shoves continued until the Page, wriggling out of the way, had moved so far down in the space that his legs stuck out beyond the furthest edge of the lowest boughs, and his head and torso were even with his Master's backside.

Here, shivering in his shirt, and receiving periodic kicks from his Master, he passed the night in shallow and broken sleep, warming himself with thoughts and dreams of all that he would receive in the Kingdom to come.

ORHAN MILOSHE lives and works in Cleveland, Ohio. *HAZAIAH'S HEAD* is his second novel. His first novel, *I AWOKE IN A HOUSE AFIRE*, was published by The Artless Dodges Press in 2010. More of his work may be found by visiting www.OrhanMiloshe.WordPress.com.

www.ingramcontent.com/pod-product-compliance
Lightning Source LLC
Chambersburg PA
CBHW050032180626
46810CB00002B/689